Wild Child

Books 1, 2 and 3

Katrina Kahler & Kaz Campbell

Copyright © KC Global Enterprises Pty Ltd

All Rights Reserved

Table of Contents

Book 1

The Initiation

Chapter One - The Welcoming

I didn't want to be stuck in the back of my parents stuffy Mercedes. Even with the window fully wound down and the air-conditioning on, it still felt like a sauna. Maybe that meant I was coming down with something. Yeah, I had to be ill, too ill to be starting some snooty girls' boarding school in the middle of nowhere.

"Dad, I don't feel well," I croaked, as I placed a hand over my sweaty forehead and gave my best-pained look.

He looked at me in the rear-view mirror with concerned eyes. He opened his mouth to say something, but I saw mom turn and glare at him.

"The school will have a nurse or something," mom muttered.

"You can't leave me there if I'm ill," I pleaded.

"In five minutes, we'll be at your new school and after we drop you off we have to rush to catch a plane home to New York, so stop being a pain," she said sternly.

It felt like my mom hated me. I was unloved, even my dad wouldn't stand up for me. "Whatever," I said under my breath, staring out of the window.

It was a typical sunny Californian day, yet my mom was as frosty as a New York's winter. I loved the summertime best of all, I mean who didn't like cute skirts and colorful bikinis? Still, there was something about New York's winter that I yearned for. Strolling through a snowy Central Park in my designer faux fur coat always felt magical.

My parents were ridiculous, I mean seriously, how could they think that leaving me at some lame boarding school was fair? Yes, okay, I'd burnt down our house, but it had been an accident. I was the one who had to live with burn marks on my face and arm, not them.

I itched at the red mark on my arm, it wasn't as fierce in the shade as it had once been, but it was still noticeable. The mark on my cheek had faded more (thankfully). I covered all the horrible scars with makeup. I knew that even with the red marks I was pretty, like really, really pretty. I was the easily the most beautiful girl in my old school. I mean Sandy was attractive, Rach okay and Susie a mere average. I was in a different league to them, it was embarrassing really.

I thought about my old friends and gave a thoughtful sigh. So okay, I guess I was going to miss them a little bit. I daydreamed about the fun I had with those girls. The sleepover when my parents pretended to attack us was the best. It was a night that none of them would ever forget.

"We're here," dad said glumly.

I stared through the window open-mouthed, they had to be kidding me. The grey-stoned building looked like something out of a period drama! Surely, they weren't actually serious, they couldn't actually think about leaving me here?

"Isn't it beautiful?" dad looked at me through the rear-view mirror with hopeful eyes. Poor dad, always the peace-maker.

"No, it's hideous," I pronounced. "It looks more like a prison or a mental asylum, where they lock up people.

"It will do you good," mom snarled. She stared at me with narrow eyes. I'd seen that look before, many times, and I knew that it meant she was really angry.

"I want to come to New York with you. Please let me come? Don't leave me in this dreadful place. I'll be good, I promise." I was begging, tears were cascading down my eyes and my hands wouldn't stop shaking.

"Sydney, you burned down my house while cooking food with an obscene number of calories in it," she shuddered as she said the word *calories*. "You don't fit in with our family. Sometimes, I wonder where you came from. I've had enough, I just can't cope with you anymore."

"Cope with me, I'm your daughter, not last season's Prada handbag!" I cried.

"Well, maybe you have gone out of fashion," she snapped back.

I dabbed at the corner of my eyes, trying to bring myself under control. I didn't care what mom said, and I didn't care about her. If anything was last season, it was her! I mean everything about her was fake…her hair, her nails, her tan. *Fake, fake, fake!*

The bronzed gates were open, and they led onto the longest driveway EVER!!! It took us past the perfectly manicured lawns. Like seriously, was this owned by the Stepford Wives or something? I rolled my eyes at the thought.

I turned and looked out of the back window as a group of girls in hideous skirts, and polo tops jogged past. A middle-aged woman in a tracksuit ran after them. She gave us a smile and a wave before she blew on the whistle around her neck.

"Come on girls, quicken up the pace," she shouted.

"Oh good, they make you do exercise. At least that should stop you from putting *any more* weight on," mom pronounced.

I turned around and slumped down into my seat. I didn't want to run across the stupid lawn in those gross sports kits. Why were my parents doing this to me? Surely forcing me to stay here was a form of child abuse? I mean, this place was like something out of a horror film.

Dad pulled up outside of the main entrance and hurried around to open the passenger door for mom. She put her oversized black-framed sunglasses on before she stepped out of the car. He opened my door and gave me a pitying smile.

"Daddy, please don't leave me here." I gave him my best angelic look.

"I'm sorry, pumpkin." He scratched at his head. "I'm sure it'll be great."

"It looks awful." I folded my arms.

"Come on." He forced a smile.

"Make me?" I snarled.

"Will you stop causing a scene," mom hissed at me.

I remained where I was. If my parents were going to insist on leaving me in this dreadful place, then they'd have to drag me out of the car.

"Get out," she hissed again before she grabbed my arm by the burn mark and pulled.

I screamed out and tried to yank it back, but she kept on pulling.

"Catherine, her arm," dad said meekly.

"Silly me, I forget," she gave me a vindictive look as she let go of my arm. "Be glad I didn't lose a nail." She studied her pink gel talons.

I reluctantly stepped out of the car and flicked back my hair. I didn't want to be stuck with *her* anyway and her stupid strict obsessive rules. New York could have them both, I would be just fine here.

Mom tottered up the entrance steps in her Gucci heels. I smirked to myself as I watched dad struggle to get my two suitcases out of the boot. Seriously, I only had two bags to last me a whole term in this place. This lame place had even lamer rules about our clothes. Apparently, we were only allowed to wear what we wanted after lessons on weekdays and on a Sunday after church. Even worse than the fact I had to wear a hideous uniform and go to church…was the fact that they had school lessons on a Saturday!!!

I left dad lugging the suitcases and followed mom into the high ceilinged, musty smelling entrance. Portraits of stern-faced looking men and women filled the walls.

"Jeez." I rolled my eyes.

It was official, this place was more like a prison than a school.

Mom didn't even comment on the portraits. Instead, she walked off towards the reception desk and dinged the bell that was on the unmanned desk. I lingered back and watched dad wheel the suitcases along the creaky wooden floor. He left the bags by the staircase and walked over to me with a sad look on his face.

"Pull yourself together," mom glared at him.

He used the back of his hand to wipe tears from his eyes and then he stared down at his feet. I rolled my eyes; this place was as pathetic as my parents were. Why didn't dad speak up and stop her from doing this to me?

A mousey-haired woman in an oversized blouse scurried out of a back room and looked at us from behind the desk.

"I assume you've been expecting me, my name is Mrs. Harding," my mom said in her poshest tone.

“Yes, yes of course,” the mousey-haired woman blushed. “I’ll let Miss Braun know you’re here.”

She fumbled around on her desk before she picked up an ancient looking cord phone. Seriously, this place really was ridiculous. I walked over to the steps and sat down on one. I looked down at my bare nails as we weren’t allowed to wear nail polish at this stupid school and then I looked over at my parents. Mom had a hand on her waist and was giving dad a stern look, no doubt his showing some emotion was annoying her, it seemed as though he couldn’t breathe without bugging her.

Maybe love wasn't like it was in the movies, maybe my parents were prime examples of what it was really like. Oh dear, I hoped they weren’t. If they were…then I was definitely going to stay single indefinitely.

I heard footsteps behind me, but I didn't turn to look. I mean, who cared? Instead, I closed my eyes in the hope that when I opened them, this whole thing would have been some lame nightmare.

Someone coughed to clear their voice, so I opened my eyes. Standing in front of me was an old woman, she was pursing at me through her wrinkled lips. I mean, as old people went, she looked okayish; her grey hair was in a neat bob and she was in a navy skirt suit. Was she one of the student’s grandmas? Was she lost?

"Yeah?" I stared back at her.

Her eyes widened in alarm.

"We do not use the word 'yeah' in this school," she announced.

I was about to tell her that it was rude to stare when my mom quickly walked over. She was doing that annoying 'fake smile' she did when she was trying to impress someone. Why was she trying to impress this old grandma?

"Good morning, I am Miss Braun, the headteacher here at St Andrews. I do hope your journey was a pleasant one?" the old woman said.

"Yes, it was most delightful." Mom kept up her posh voice.

"Get me out of here," I muttered under my breath.

"Excuse me?" The old woman looked at me. "You said something."

"No, I didn't say anything." I gave my sweetest smile.

"Indeed," she muttered. "Please, follow me," she gave a wave of her wrinkled hand and led us up the stairs.

I traipsed after my parents up the wooden staircase. Every step I took seemed to creak that bit louder. Why couldn't this building just fall down already and then I could go home? *Home,* the word repeated in my head. I didn't have a home, not anymore. I felt like an unwanted, deserted orphan. All alone in the world with nobody to love me. Surely, Dad would come to my rescue soon. Especially after seeing how decrepit the building was and how dreadful the principal looked.

She led us into the world's worst office. It smelt of old people, and the desk was full of weird bronzed ornaments. My parents sat down in front of her desk, but I remained over by the door. The old woman was staring at me again, she seriously needed to quit it, I felt like I was on trial or something. I walked over to the oak chair that was next to my dad and looked down at it. Talk about ancient, she really needed to update this place, it was like something out of a *Dracula movie.*

"Ahem," she coughed. "I think you forget something."

I looked at her and resisted the urge to roll my eyes. How could she accuse me of forgetting something? She was the one who lived in the dark ages.

"Oh, um, can I sit down?" I asked.

"No, you can't sit down, but you may sit down," she replied.

It was official, this woman was bonkers!

"We value the correct use of English here at St Andrews," she said to my parents.

"How…quaint," my mom said. She was still fake smiling. And I've never heard her use a word like quaint before. Such an actress!

I sat down on the chair that was no doubt older than me and looked at the woman who was probably older than Dumbledore.

"Young lady, your attitude will not be tolerated here. It needs to change and quickly." Miss Braun glared at me.

Dad looked uneasy as he loosened the tie that mom had made him wear. Mom gave a gleeful smirk, she wanted me to be punished. Mom was never going to forgive me for burning down our last house. She was never going to love me like a mother was meant to love her daughter.

My eyes focused on the gold locket that hung from Miss Braun's wrinkled neck. I shook my head and looked away. By the looks of this place, I wouldn't have been surprised if she used her pendant to hypnotize all of her students. I imagined her turning all her students into snotty-nosed clones.

"Here at St Andrews, we have a strict code of rules to follow. Rule number one, the correct uniform must be worn at all times. Skirts must come to within 10 cms above your knees and shirts must be neatly tucked in. Rule number two, lateness will not be tolerated, you must take responsibility for your own time-management and make sure that you arrive promptly to all lessons.

Rule number three, you are not permitted to leave the school grounds without permission.

Ha-ha, I felt like telling her that rules were made to be broken. I smirked to myself. She continued to list off more rules, but I stopped listening. This place was awful, and I was already planning on how to get out of here. What were they going to do, expel me? They'd be doing me a favor if they did, as then I wouldn't be stuck here anymore.

"Do you understand?" Miss Braun was staring at me.

"What?" I said.

"I see what you mean," Miss Braun sighed, as she looked at my mom. "Don't worry, in six months you'll have a changed daughter, one who isn't rude."

My mom smiled, and I rolled my eyes, of course, my mom had told this fossil of a woman terrible things about me. To her, I was just a problem child, a liability. Even if I did change into a perfectly dull person, I still doubted that I'd be good enough for her. Anyway, it's not like I care anymore, not one little bit.

I bit on my lip and twisted a strand of my hair around my finger.

"Would you like to accompany Sydney to her room?" Miss Braun asked.

"No." My mom jumped to her feet. "She'll be fine. Besides, we have a plane to catch."

She leaned over me so that I could smell her overpowering perfume and gave me an awkward hug. I sat there rigid, willing her to stop. She air-kissed each of my cheeks then let go of me.

"Bye have a lovely time," she gave a wave of her hand before she strutted out of the room.

I stood up at the same time as dad did. Before I fully knew what was going on, he'd wrapped his arms around me and was sobbing into my hair.

"Daddy, please get me out of here," I whispered in his ear.

"I'll try," he whispered back. "Be a good girl."

His phone in his pocket began to ring and he pulled away from me and answered it. "Yes, I'm coming now."

"That was your mother, I'd better go," he gave me a knowing look and rolled his eyes.

I managed to force a smile and then I watched him leave the room. Now it was just the old woman and me...great.

"Follow me Sydney, I'll show you to your room?" she announced.

Finally, I'd get some time to myself in my bedroom. There better be a comfy mattress and a decent shower in the bathroom. For an old person, Miss Braun walked briskly, and I struggled to keep up with her.

"Stop dawdling," she said sternly, as she waited for me at the corner of the corridor.

I followed her along the corridor and then she stopped in front of a wooden door and knocked on it. Age had seriously got to this woman, else why else would she be knocking on the door to my room?

"Come in," a girl's voice shouted from within.

She opened the door, and I followed her into the room. I looked around open-mouthed, there were four uncomfortable looking single beds and four desks stuffed into the average sized room. Worse still, there were three other girls in there.

"Girls, this is Sydney, your new roommate. I'm in no doubt that you'll make her feel welcome," Miss Braun commented.

"Of course, Miss Braun," said a girl with long blonde hair. She gave a sickly-sweet smile.

"There must be some mistake! I can't be expected to share a bedroom!" I looked at Miss Braun. This day just kept getting worse! I've always had my own bedroom and privacy!

The other girls all laughed, but I didn't see what was funny about this situation.

"Goodbye girls." Miss Braun shook her head as she left the room.

I stood there feeling extremely annoyed and frustrated. How dare she ignore my question, I was entitled to my own room.

"That's your bed over there," the blonde girl pointed to the bed furthest away from the door. "The one by the bathroom." She smirked.

The other girls both sniggered.

"Whatever." I walked over to the bed and sat down on it.

"I'm Harper," said the blonde girl, giving a devious smile. "That's Brianna." She pointed to a girl with short brown hair who giggled as she looked at me. "And that's Taylor," she gestured to a girl with auburn hair that was tied up.

"Hi." Taylor blushed.

"Hi." I rolled my eyes. I didn't really feel like small talk, but I suppose I had to make an effort.

"I'm in charge around here." Harper smirked. "Don't you forget it."

"Whatever." I sighed. This was not going to be easy. Taylor seemed okay, but Harper, she was going to be a small challenge.

"There are rules here," Harper announced.

"Yeah, I know. I've already been told them."

"Not those rules, *our* rules. You can't tell anyone about them, but you have to follow them if you want to be accepted. See it as an initiation to prove your worth. Pass, and we'll be your friends, fail, and we'll make sure your stay is a living hell, you'll be a nobody."

I stood up and looked Harper up-and-down. She was pretty I guess, and she clearly thought that she was in charge. I didn't take orders from anyone, I was a leader, not a follower. I was about to tell Harper this, but then Brianna came and sat down next to me.

"Heya," she giggled as she swung out her legs. "Do you have a boyfriend?"

"Hi," I forced a smile. "Nah, I don't have a boyfriend."

"Me neither," she giggled again.

"We're at an all-girls school Bree, where are you going to find a boyfriend?" Harper rolled her eyes. I wasn't sure if Harper was annoyed by Brianna's dizziness or the fact that she was trying to be nice to me.

Brianna giggled before she hummed happily to herself.

I looked over at that Taylor girl, she was sitting on her bed flipping through her notebook.

"Taylor, aren't you going to talk to the new girl?" Harper stared at her.

Taylor looked up with alarm and then dropped her notebook. Harper smirked at this and Taylor looked flustered. What was with this Harper girl and why did people find her so intimidating? I watched as Taylor bent down and picked up her notebook.

"Yeah, um, hi," Taylor spluttered.

"Hi," I replied.

"You've already said hi. Why not try something more original." Harper smirked at Taylor. "Like, welcome to St Andrews. Enjoy getting up super early, going to church on a Sunday, having zero space for yourself. Oh, and because you're new, you're lowest on the pecking order and have to follow our orders."

"Yeah, the initiation, you've already told me. Come up with something more original," I rolled my eyes.

Harper looked furious, but she didn't say anything. She may have acted like she was the top-dog, but she was no match for me.

Harper

People need to understand that I am in charge around here. I mean, what do they expect? After all, my dad's a heart surgeon, and my mom's a top-level business analyst. Last year, my parents were named in Who Magazine in the top 100 influential couples. Of course, I'm smart like they are, I'm pretty too, actually I’m told that I’m gorgeous. I'd rate myself a nine out of ten which makes me far prettier than the majority of the girls here. Then again, most of them are pretty ugly.

I may be a leader, but I think I'm a fair person. I mean, as long as people don't cross me, then I’m kind enough to them.

I was in *my* room staring at the new girl. Yeah okay, so she was prettier than the others, and she didn’t seem fazed by me, which was strange. It had been funny when she’d freaked out when she realized she wouldn't get her own room. Like seriously, where did she think she was? This wasn't a five-star resort, this was Saint Andrews.

I was already sick of her smart remarks and couldn't wait to see the smile wiped from her face. She needed to accept that she was the new girl. Therefore, she needed to do *whatever* I wanted.

"Sydney, if you want to fit in here then you have to pass nine tests. Basically, you'll be like a cat with nine lives, my advice is that you don't mess them up. You'll find that this school can be a very lonely place when you don't have any friends."

I smiled when I saw her gulp.

"Rule one- We have a serious hierarchy, and you don't step out of line, ever! I'm the boss, and you are my new slave."

Sydney snorted on hearing this.

"For the next week, you will do everything I tell you to."

Sydney looked at me unfazed. Usually, when I told someone this, they looked terrified, but not her, she was sitting there with her back straight, and her head held high. I was pretty impressed, but I wasn't going to let her know this.

"The first part of your slave initiation is to serve me my food for a week. The older girls give out the food in the cafeteria, your job is to fetch my tray of food before you get your own."

"You can get your own food," Sydney said as she frowned at me.

"We'll see about that." I gave a sly smile.

***

Lunchtime arrived, and I sat down at my table in the cafeteria and watched as Sydney lined up in the queue.

This was going to be fun, I thought to myself.

Some of the older girls were in charge of dishing out the food. When Sydney got to the front of the queue, Meg, a sassy seventeen-year-old looked over at me, and I gave her a nod back. Soon, Sydney was begrudgingly walking over to me.

"There!" She slammed the tray of food down in front of me.

"Hmmm, a bit slow and less of the attitude next time," I said sarcastically.

Sydney muttered something under her breath before she walked back over to the front of the queue.

I smirked to myself as I watched Meg order her to the back of the line. I put a forkful of potato in my mouth as I watched her sulk and walk to the back. Watching the new girl squirm was the best entertainment, even better than going to the movies.

Brianna and Taylor sat down next to me and looked over at a mad looking Sydney.

"She looks so annoyed," I sniggered.

"Yeah, she does," Taylor replied.

"She's pretty tough," Brianna commented.

"She's not that smart and she's not pretty," I muttered.

"You're prettier," Taylor added.

"You're super pretty Harper, but she is beautiful," Brianna giggled before she popped a carrot into her mouth.

I tried to hide my annoyance, I mean, what did Brianna know anyway, she was such an air-head. Sydney marched over to us and plonked her tray of food down next to Brianna. She didn't look at any of us, she just started eating.

"I can't wait till we all get boyfriends." Brianna tilted her head. "We could go on a group date."

"You're not going to find a boyfriend in this place," I replied. Brianna's obsession with finding a boyfriend was becoming irritating.

"I know that. I meant in the future," she replied.

Brianna could be okay sometimes, but her stupidity tended to annoy me. And talking about annoying…Amy was walking over to me with that stupid toothed smile of hers. Seriously, that girl was all teeth, it made me want to shudder.

“Heya,” Amy said, as she sat down next Taylor.

I didn’t say anything to her. She was part of my group and all, but she was so boring.

“Hi, you must be the new girl?” She smiled at Sydney.

“Well that’s obvious,” I said under my breath.

“Yeah, I’m Sydney.”

“I'm Amy, I'm in the room next door with Zoe, she's a new girl too. Well, she started at the beginning of the term. How do you like it here?" Amy asked.

“Amy, she’s been here for a couple of hours.” I rolled my eyes. “How could she possibly know what it’s like?”

"Actually, I've got a pretty good impression," Sydney replied.

"Amy, do you have a boyfriend?" Brianna asked.

"No." She shook her head.

Was this what my life had come to? I was queen bee around here, the original wild child, yet right now I was stuck with dumb-and-dumber going on about irrelevant nonsense. I was too good for this place.

"This uniform is so itchy," Sydney pulled at the collar of her shirt.

"Get used to it, you'll be practically living in the thing." I smirked.

"Great," she muttered. "In my last school, we could wear what we wanted to."

"Sydney, why is your arm red?" Amy pointed at it.

"I must have knocked it or something," she quickly moved her arm so that it was mostly beneath the table.

I noticed how uncomfortable she looked. Finally, this girl had a weakness.

"I'm always doing that too, I'm so clumsy," Amy replied.

"Yeah, and you suck at hockey. We lost to Ivy Close because you fell over, remember?" I glared at Amy.

Amy looked embarrassed, but as usual, she didn't say anything back.

"Hockey?" Sydney raised an eyebrow. "Seriously?"

"Yeah, hockey," I sneered. "Get used to it, things are very different around here."

Sydney smiled at me before she bit into her apple.

***

The next two days were hilarious. Every time we went to the cafeteria, Sydney tried to get her tray first, but every time Meg and the other girls in charge refused to give it to her. What was even better was the fact that when she did get her food she came and sat with us. She didn't have anyone else, it was us or no one and trust me, if she didn't pass the initiation then she'd end up with no one.

You may think I'm a mean person, maybe I am. What you have to understand is that it's tough here at boarding school. There is no room for cry-babies or the weak. I'm really doing Sydney a favor. Besides, it wasn't like I was starving her or anything, she just had to get my food first and then she could eat.

Compared to the other girls I could tell that Sydney was different. She didn't cry herself to sleep or say whatever she thought I wanted to hear. It was clear that she absolutely hated being ordered around by me, which I took great delight in.

I was sitting at my table in the cafeteria examining my nails as I waited for Sydney to bring over my lunch. *Slam!* Slimy mashed-up pumpkin splattered all over me. I looked up to see Sydney grinning back at me.

"I hope you like being hungry." I sneered.

I flicked a piece of pumpkin at her, but she dodged out of its way. The head of the cafeteria walked over to us carrying a tray and held it out to Sydney.

“Here you are Sydney, just what your doctor ordered.”

“Thank you so much,” she gave a sickly-sweet smile, as she took the tray from her.

I looked at her as she sat down opposite me.

“How?” I asked.

Okay, I had to admit that I was impressed. This Sydney girl was pretty smart.

She stuck her fork into a piece of pasta, put it into her mouth and chewed slowly on it.

“So, I drew red dots on my arms and face. Then I went to the head of the cafeteria with a note I forged from my doctor making out that I had severe nut and egg allergies and that my food needed to be prepared separately.”

I laughed out loudly. Okay, this meant that from now on I'd have to get my own food, but I had to give it to her, she was far more cunning and sneaky than I thought she was capable of being.

Chapter Two - What Privacy

Privacy is different at boarding school. Back home I'd had no brothers or sisters to run into my room and jump on my bed. I'd had a massive bedroom all to myself and my own bathroom. Here I had to share a wardrobe with the other girls. I mean seriously, who shares a wardrobe?

I just wanted a moment to myself, some peace and quiet, but they never stopped. Even at night time, I couldn't get any peace as Brianna breathed loudly during her sleep. It was like sleeping next to a railway line, constant and extremely annoying. Taylor's bed creaked every time she moved and that was all through the night. This place was ridiculous, and I hated it here.

It was the end of the school day, and I wanted to change out of this horrible uniform and into something cool. The other girls were all sitting on their beds, like come on girls! Couldn't they give me some privacy?

"Please, can you step outside so I can get changed?" I asked them.

"You've got a lot to learn Sydney." Brianna giggled.

"Yeah." Taylor laughed.

Harper didn't even look up from her book. I wanted to grab the thing and throw it across the room, but I resisted the temptation, after-all, I did have to share a room with these girls.

"Well, you could at least close your eyes."

Harper put the book down and signaled to the other girls to follow her. Soon all three of them had circled around me. I sighed before I picked the pile of clothes off my bed and walked towards the bathroom. Harper whizzed past me and stood in the doorway with her arms pressed against either side of the wall.

"You can't change in there, someone might want to go to the toilet," Harper said.

"Well, it's lucky that no one is in there then, isn't it?" I smirked.

Harper moved her arm as Taylor darted into the bathroom, slamming the door behind her. Harper was glaring at me, and I needed to figure out how to play this and fast, should I wait or be bold? Hey, I wasn't a 'waiting around' kind of girl, so I threw my clothes back onto my bed and started unbuttoning my shirt. I took it off along with my gross school skirt and threw them both onto the floor. I stood there in my underwear with my hands on my hips.

"Have a good look, I know you both want to admire perfection," I said confidently.

Harper and Brianna both burst into laughter. Whatever...neither of them bothered me. I changed into my black pants and cute pink vest top and then bent down and picked my uniform up.

Harper and Brianna were still laughing. I rolled my eyes, they were so pathetic.

"Taylor, you can come out now," Harper shouted.

Taylor walked out of the bathroom and gave me an apologetic look. She was too gutless to say sorry and gave me an 'are you okay' signal with her hand when Harper wasn't watching.

I looked away from her, she'd chosen to be Harper's sheepdog. If she had expected me to give her pitying looks back, she was even more foolish than I first thought.

I stormed into the bathroom and into the toilet cubicle and shut the door. I sat down on the toilet, relieved that I could finally get some alone time. Suddenly, the door burst open and Harper stood there smirking at me. Panic washed over me, but I tried my best not to show it.

"I didn't say you could close the door, Sydney." She sneered.

"Fine, I'll keep it open." I tried to sound unfazed.

I hopped off the toilet, brushed past her and walked over to the basin. I hummed to myself as I washed my hands. I felt embarrassed, but there was no way that I was going to let Harper see that she'd got to me.

"Seeya Harper," I shouted, as I left the bathroom.

I needed to be away from those girls, so I left the bedroom and walked out into the corridor. I didn't really know where I was going as this place was a maze but anywhere was better than being stuck in there with them.

You're strong Sydney. You can do this, I told myself. *You're better than those stupid girls.*

I hated this place, the corridors felt stifling and it smelt of old people. Miss Braun was surely about one-hundred-years old, so it made sense that the whole place smelt like an old people's home.

I missed my old home and my old friends. They never treated me like Harper and her stupid friends did, instead they had hung onto my every word. I'm a leader, not a follower, and Harper needed to get used to it.

I stopped walking and looked around me. I'd been so distracted by those stupid girls that I'd walked into a part of the building that I didn't recognize. I walked along the corridor and came to a dead end, so I turned around and tried another route. This place was ridiculous, I swear the landings were moving like the staircases did in Hogwarts. Sighing, I crouched down next to the wall and hugged my legs.

I hated this school. I hated having to share a room with those horrid girls. Most of all, I hated my parents for leaving me here. I buried my head in my hands and tried to imagine that I was back in Venice Beach with Sandy, Rach, and Susie.

"You're not meant to be in this part of the building," a male voice said.

I looked up and saw a slim, middle-aged man in blue overalls staring at me, a hammer grasped in his hand. The panic began to set in, not only was I lost in this decrepit school, but now I was stuck with some weird man who was probably going to bludgeon me to death with his hammer. Would my parents even care if I was murdered or would they be pleased that they'd never have to see me again?

He noticed my alarm and then looked down at his hand and saw the hammer. "Oh, sorry," he muttered. "Miss Braun asked me to move a picture, I didn't mean to scare you."

"You didn't scare me," I said as assertively as I could.

"Ah, okay. You really shouldn't be here though."

"I don't know where I am," I sighed. "I'm new here, and I'm lost."

"Ah," he scratched at his head. "I suppose this place is like a maze. I'll show you back to the main part if you'd like?"

“Thanks,” I forced a smile. “But I’ll be okay.”

"Dad, where do you want this?" a boy with messy brown hair walked around the corner, he was holding a portrait. “Oh, hi,” he said when he noticed me.

“Hi,” I smiled back. This boy was cute, really cute!

“I’ll be with you in a minute.”

The boy gave him a nod to his dad and took another look at me and then walked off carrying the portrait.

“I didn’t think boys were allowed here?” I murmured.

"Elliot's my son," the man scratched at his head again. “I'm Mr. Meuler, the janitor here. Anyway, are you sure I can’t show you how to get back?”

“I’ll find my way, thank you.” I smiled.

"Ah, okay. Well, you need to go up there," he pointed up the corridor. "Then take a left and then a sharp right, then keep on walking and you should come out by the portrait of Miss Hemmingway, she was the first headmistress here, you can't miss her."

"Okay," I jumped to my feet and started to walk off. "And thanks," I looked back and smiled at them.

Why didn't this school have signs up or something? I felt like I was walking in circles. By the time I found myself standing in front of a portrait with Miss Hemmingway written beneath it, I was exhausted. I gave a relieved sigh. The portrait was massive, it was at least three times my width and the woman painted on it was stern-faced and wearing a black cape and a royal blue hat with three peacock feathers sticking up from it.

This place is ridiculous, I thought to myself.

"You should be in your room doing your homework," a voice behind me said.

I turned around to see Meg from the cafeteria standing there. She was still in her school uniform, and her green prefect badge glistened on her shirt.

"I'm on my way there now," I replied.

"I won't give you detention this time," she stared at me with frosty blue eyes. "But that's only because you're new."

"Gee, thanks," I muttered under my breath.

I walked off feeling fed-up. I hated this school, I hated my parents, I hated everything!

"By the way, that whole stunt you pulled with Harper's tray, yeah, that was pretty clever."

I looked back at her, she was smirking at me. Maybe this Meg girl wasn't so bad after all.

"Oh that, that was nothing." I grinned before I flicked my hair behind my back and walked off.

***

The other girls were talking amongst themselves as they got ready for bed. I didn't want to join in, I just wanted to get into my bed and dream that I wasn't stuck in this nightmare.

"Good night, Harper." I smirked at her. "Sweet dreams."

I hopped into my bed, faced the wall and pulled the cover over me. Okay, so admittedly I wasn't that tired, but staring at a wall was better than engaging in conversation with those idiots. Sharing a room totally sucked and should have been made illegal. This room was far too small for four girls to be in it and don't even get me started on the bathroom. There's no way my mom would have slept in here, yet she was happy to let her only child be stuck here.

"It's such a pain to have to share a room with another girl, especially this one," Harper said loudly.

"Don't worry Harper, she won't fit in here, and her mommy and daddy will come and take her away." Brianna giggled.

"To a school for losers and ugly brats." Harper pretended to play the violin.

"Yeah, she'd fit in there." Brianna giggled some more.

"I can't wait until tomorrow when she has to be my slave again. It must be so humiliating for her having all of the other girls laughing at her and thinking she's so pathetic," Harper said sarcastically.

"Will you two shut up, I'm trying to sleep," Taylor complained.

"What was that? Did the mouse speak? Squeak, squeak, squeak." Harper sneered. "Don't get too big for your boots Taylor, or you can be my slave too."

Taylor let out a loud sigh and then fell silent. I closed my eyes and tried to sleep, but my mind wouldn't switch off. Then there were the little sounds that I wasn't used to. The rustling of a bedcover, someone coughing, the sounds of breathing.

I hated my mom for leaving me here, and I hated my dad even more for letting her.

***

I woke up to Harper standing over me, a large pile of books in her hand.

"W-what," I mumbled.

I rubbed my eyes and yawned. It was far too early for this, I wanted to go back to sleep, not deal with Harper and her painful followers.

"Morning slave, today you can carry my books for me," she dropped them onto the floor beside my bed.

I jumped out of bed and stared straight back at her.

"Carry them yourself!" I shouted.

I grabbed my toiletry bag and marched into the bathroom. I was brushing my teeth when Brianna barged in, stuck her tongue out at me and then ran off. I rolled my eyes and carried on brushing. Suddenly, the door opened, and this time Taylor came in, she stood there awkwardly and then left. I spat out the toothpaste and then looked into the mirror that was above the sink where I could see Harper's reflection. She was leaning in the doorway, her arms were folded, and there was a smirk on her face.

"Can't you bare to be away from me for even a minute?" I said, raising an eyebrow as I turned and looked at her.

"This is more my bathroom than yours as I've been here longer, so if I want to use it, then I will."

"Whatever," I shrugged.

I grabbed my toiletry bag and brushed past her. Seriously, what kind of establishment didn't have locks on the bathroom doors? Apparently, it was a health and safety rule. Well, it was a ridiculous one!

As I changed into my uniform, the other girls were sniggering at me. I brushed my hair and tied it up into a high ponytail and then I looked around for my hair clips.

"Looking for something?" Harper asked.

I looked over at her, and that's when I saw my sparkly hair clips in her hair. As much as I wanted to go over to her and yank them out…I decided against it.

"Whatever, I don't need them anyway." I gave a sarcastic smile.

"They look better on me anyway. Everything looks better on me." Harper was posing like a model.

I maintained my smile as I sorted my books out. She was pretty, but I knew that I was more beautiful. She was smart, but I was smarter. She may have been a leader for now, but if I had my way, that was soon going to change.

"Hurry up, or you'll make us late for breakfast." Harper glared at me. "And carry my books or you'll have to sit on a table by yourself."

I looked down at the collapsed pile of textbooks on the floor and sighed.

"No, you can carry them yourself." I glared back at Harper before I left the room.

"You'll regret that," she shouted after me.

I wasn't Harper's servant, she could carry her own books and collect her own tray. She wasn't the queen, she was just some stuck-up kid in his awful school. Besides, I didn't want to sit with them anyway, I'd much rather sit by myself.

As soon as I'd walked into the cafeteria one of the cooks appeared and passed me a tray with my breakfast on it. I thanked her before I headed towards an empty table near the back of the room (purposely as far away from Harper's group as possible). A group of older girls whizzed past me and placed their trays down on my table. They all frowned at me.

"Whatever." I rolled my eyes. I walked over to a table where only two girls sat and placed my tray by the seat furthest away from them.

"You can't sit there," one of the girls said, glaring at me.

"But no one's sitting here," I replied.

"We don't care, you can't sit there," the other girl said.

"You need to move."

"No." I pulled in my chair and folded my arms.

One of the girls leaned over and knocked over my glass.

Orange juice splattered onto my shirt and drenched my breakfast. I was well aware that everyone in the cafeteria was staring at me, I was their sole focus, but I kept my cool.

“I wasn't hungry anyway,” I said before I stood up and walked confidently across the room.

As I passed Harper's table, I could hear her and the others laughing. I kept my gaze away from her as I left the room. I hurried back to my bedroom and changed my shirt, then I sat on the edge of my bed and sighed to myself. I was not a victim, and it was about time that Harper and her pathetic little group realized that. It was time that I showed them exactly what Sydney Harding was capable of.

***

Classes were so boring. The teachers were all nearly as decrepit as Miss Braun, and I’d resorted to eating my lunch in the hallway adjacent to the cafeteria (but if you tell anyone about that I will stick chewing gum in your hair). What kept me going was the knowledge that I was going to get revenge, and I couldn't wait. That evening, after enduring Harper and her friends’ immature comments and constant nagging, I changed into my nightdress in front of them. All three of them were looking at me, Brianna was giggling, and Harper had her usual smug smirk on her face.

“Take a good look, I know you’re all jealous because I’m so much better looking than all of you.” I gave them a twirl.

“As if!” Harper rolled her eyes.

“If you were that beautiful you would have a boyfriend,” Brianna said.

“You don’t have one either,” I replied.

“So!” Brianna shrugged. “I could get one if I wanted.”

"Yeah." I smirked. "Sure, you could."

I grabbed my toiletry bag off my bedside table and walked into the bathroom. I quickly opened the cabinet under the sink where I'd already put a bucket filled with water. I lugged it out, lifted it up and carefully balanced it on top of the partially open toilet door. I sat on the toilet and waited. I heard laughter followed by footsteps, the door swung open, and the bucket tipped onto Harper and absolutely soaked her. She let out a loud squeal and jumped back.

Brianna and Taylor raced into the room to see what all the commotion was about. When they saw Harper standing there all wet, they both burst out laughing.

"What are you staring at?" Harper said through gritted teeth.

"I'm sorry Harper, you just look so funny." Brianna giggled.

"You," Harper pointed a finger at me. "I'll get you for this."

"It's easy, don't walk in on me when I'm in the bathroom." I gave her a sickly-sweet smile and turned on the shower. Harper stormed out.

After my shower, I walked out of the room feeling good about myself, a feeling that soon evaporated when I caught Brianna and Taylor snooping through my bedside cabinet.

"Get out of there!" I stormed over to it and slammed the door shut.

"We were only looking," Brianna shook her head. "Chill out."

I grabbed the book off my bedside table and lay down on my bed. I couldn't concentrate on reading, but I flipped the pages at the right amount of time intervals to give the impression that I was.

Ten minutes later Harper appeared wrapped in a towel, her wet nightdress in her hand.

"I wanted a shower anyway." She stared at me with a look of hate.

"Yeah, sure you did," I replied before I went back to pretending to read my book.

***

I woke up stupidly early so that I could use the bathroom before the others. The pokey shower was nothing like my walk-in-one back at home, and there was no bathtub. At least I wasn't interrupted, it seemed as though my bucket stunt had worked. I wrapped my wet hair up in a towel and then changed into my uniform in the bathroom. I walked out of there to find Harper prancing around the room in my designer purple strappy top.

"Look at me, I'm Sydney, and I'm a loser." She swished her hair behind her back.

"Take it off!" I glared at her.

"I think I'm so amazing and beautiful because my mommy and daddy buy me whatever I want, but really, I'm just a loser."

"I said, take it off!" I continued to stare at her.

I noticed something sparkling in her ears. Earrings, *my* silver earrings.

"Take them out," I said through gritted teeth.

"Don't be such a scrooge. Remember rule two, privacy is different in boarding school. What's yours is mine and what's mine is mine," Harper grinned. "Relax, you can get your trashy stuff back later."

Harper and Brianna high-fived each other and then they both walked over to the wardrobe and started pulling out *my* clothes. Harper waved Taylor over, she paused and gave me an apologetic look before she joined them. I watched as all three of them tried my expensive clothes on. I bit down on my lip and tried to keep an unfazed exterior.

"How do I look?" Brianna posed in my check print skirt.

"Like you escaped from the Scotland. It does belong to Sydney, so what do you expect." Harper sneered.

"Now this is nice," Harper pulled my black t-shirt on over her head. "It's just a shame it's so big," she tugged at the sparse material.

Keep cool. Keep cool, I told myself. I didn't say anything to them, even though I felt livid.

When were these girls going to learn that messing with me was a really bad idea?

***

I was sat in the assembly hall next to this weird girl called Zoe and some girl with terrible forehead acne. I stared at my nails hoping that they'd both get the hint that I didn't want to engage in conversation. The teachers all walked in, and everyone stood up. The teachers seemed to take ages to step up onto the stage and sit down. Miss Braun walked out to the front of the stage and looked out at us.

"Thank you, girls. Please take your seats."

Finally, I thought to myself, as I sat down. Miss Braun started rambling on about some school rubbish. I don't know what she was going on about, as I wasn't listening. Instead, I was staring at the back of Harper's head and wondering how I could get my revenge. I needed a devious plan, something genius that would get her into heaps of trouble.

Miss Crombie, the snooty-nosed hall director, walked over to Miss Braun and started talking about some boring geography field trip. That's when I noticed a diamond necklace glistening around her neck. I knew some girls who wouldn't be able to resist something that sparkly.

***

For the next few days, I worked out Miss Crombie's general routine. Her office was on the first floor, not far from the main entrance. She spent most of her time in there, except when she was at lunch and meetings. The main thing I learned about Miss Crombie was that she was boring and really annoying. Work, eat, meetings, work, eat, meetings…yawn! I was walking past her office for the fifth time that day and starting to think that I'd have to think up a new plan when her office door swung open. She walked out of it wearing a horrible white dress and clutching a tennis racket. I noticed how for once her neck was bare, she'd taken off the necklace.

"Haven't you got homework to do?" She glared at me.

"I've just been to the library, Miss." I held up the history textbook that I'd loaned out earlier (I knew the importance of a good cover story). "I'm on my way to do it now." I smiled at her.

"No leaving your room during study hours. I'll let you off this once because you're new here," she announced. "Now, hop along, I can't stand dawdlers."

I nodded and then walked off up the corridor. I turned my head to check that she'd gone before I spun around and quickly headed over to her office door. Through my sleuth skills, I'd learned that she never locked it, so I sneaked into her office and closed the door behind me. It was a dark pine overload, the bookcase, antique looking desk and chairs were all dark pine. There were a couple of framed pictures of flowers in vases, one had white lilies and the other daffodils. I noticed how she didn't have any actual flowers in her office and thought that this was odd. Maybe she was allergic to them, or perhaps she only liked them in picture form, not in reality?

I walked over to her desk, placed my book down on it and then started to rummage through her desk cupboard. All I found were neatly stacked paperwork and perfectly lined pens.

"Seriously," I said under my breath. This woman really

needed to loosen up.

I checked her handbag that was underneath her desk, but the necklace wasn't in there. I looked around the room, trying to figure out where to look next when I noticed a wooden box (dark pine of course) on top of her desk. I lifted the lid, and the diamond necklace glistened back at me.

"Bingo." I grinned, as I snatched it and then closed the box.

I made sure that it was safely placed in my skirt pocket, grabbed my book then walked over to the door. I slowly opened it and peered out into the corridor, empty. I arrived back at my room to find the three girls rummaging through my stuff, again! I slumped down onto my bed and completely ignored them.

"2003 called, it wants its top back," Harper laughed, as she held up my emerald green crop top.

"No wonder she doesn't have a boyfriend," Brianna said sounding like a wound-up Barbie doll.

"Now, this is okay." Harper put on my red hooded top and zipped it up. "I mean, I'd wear it to lounge around in."

She walked over to her bedside drawer and pulled a packet of potato chips out of it and then she sat down on Taylor's bed and ate them so that crumbs fell onto my top and Taylor's bed. Neither Taylor or I said anything, but I could see the annoyance in Taylor's eyes. At least I was biding my time before I got my own back, Taylor had no backbone. She let Harper walk all over her because she was too afraid to stand up to her. She deserved to have chips all over her bed cover.

"It's such a shame I can't get my servant to do my homework. Then again, my grades would slip if I did that, as nobody is as smart as me," Harper said, as she brushed the crumbs off her and onto Taylor's bed.

We all sat at our desks and started our homework. Time seemed to drag on, as it always did in this place. Finally, 6 o'clock arrived signaling the end of study time.

The other three girls immediately stood up from their desks and rushed out of the room. I remained behind, I checked out the corridor first to make sure that they'd definitely gone before I walked over to my bedside cabinet and took out my jewelry box. I took out a few ring boxes and then I took Miss Crombie's necklace from my skirt pocket and placed it in the jewelry box. I put the ring boxes back in it, closed the lid and then put it away.

With a smile on my face, I left the room and made my way to dinner.

The new girl wasn't in the cafeteria, no doubt she was still in the bedroom crying because she has no friends. I was currently wearing her t-shirt, and she had nowhere to eat her dinner. I pictured her sitting on her bed hungry and sad, and I couldn't help but smirk to myself. You probably think I'm really mean, but I'm not. Boarding school is tough, really tough. I'm doing her a favor, she should be thanking me.

I was just finishing off my rhubarb crumble when Sydney walked into the cafeteria. One of the cooks bought her dinner over to her, and she walked confidently over to an empty table in the Senior's section. It wasn't long before a couple of the older kids went over to her and made it clear to her that she wasn't welcome there. Sydney ignored them and began to eat. I'll give her credit, that girl had courage. One of the girls grabbed Sydney's dessert bowl and walked off with it. Sydney just shrugged and then carried on eating her food.

I smiled to myself as I shook my head. That girl was something all right, she had spirit, which I liked. I was so used to everyone cowering down to me and doing exactly what I asked them to. Sydney was different, she wasn't afraid of me. I could have sent some other kids over to torment her, but I decided to leave her alone this time.

***

The next morning, while Sydney was in the bathroom, I ordered the others to search through her draws with me. Brianna grabbed her jewelry box and took out a gold ring and stuck it on her pinky.

"Ooooh, I like this," she cooed.

Taylor was more reserved, but then again, what's new. That girl was so boring, half the time I forgot she was there.

"Put this on," I shoved a charm bracelet into Taylor's hand.

She looked hesitant before she placed it around her wrist and struggled with the clasp. I rolled my eyes before I fastened it for her. I rummaged through the jewelry box, I guess she had some pretty nice things, although my collection was way better. My dad bought me a one-of-a-kind tanzanite bracelet for my birthday, but I wasn't stupid enough to bring it to school. *Oooh,* my eyes widened as I spotted a sparkly necklace. I lifted it up to study it more closely before I put it around my neck and moved my hair out of the way so that Brianna could fasten it.

"That's glitzy," Brianna said.

"I know right, Sydney's going to be furious when she sees me in."

"She so is," Brianna giggled.

I forced a smile, sometimes it was so taxing having to deal with Miss Giggly and Miss Mouse. I sat down on Sydney's bed and waited for her to come out of the bathroom. When she did, she looked straight at her necklace that glistened around my neck.

"Sydney, is something wrong?" I asked, smiling.

"No, everything's fine." She gave a forced smile.

I was going to give it back to her, eventually, I just wanted to make her sweat first.

"So, we have cross-country today," I swirled the necklace back-and-forth. "Try not to fall over in the mud this time Taylor."

Taylor blushed which made me smirk. She really was so pathetic, she let me walk all over her.

"Taylor, can you carry my English textbook for me?"

Taylor gave an awkward look and then she was silent while she processed this. "Sure," she said hesitantly.

"Well, go on then," I gestured over to it. "I haven't got all day."

Taylor scurried over to my book and picked it up. I resisted the urge to laugh-out-loud, she was such a mouse, squeak, squeak, squeak. I also resisted the urge to squeak at her. I led the way to breakfast with Brianna by my side and Taylor just behind us. Sydney was further back but who cares? I didn't want her walking with me anyway, she'd ruin my image.

Miss Crombie was standing in the corridor, she looked flustered as she spoke to Miss Braun. There was a rumor going around that her partner had left her for his yoga coach so maybe she was upset over that? Pathetic, whichever man was lucky enough to be chosen by me would never have the audacity to go off with someone else. I mean she wasn't entirely unattractive, but with her narrow-framed glasses and too-tight long beige skirt, she did look like a confused librarian.

"Morning Miss Braun, Miss Crombie." I gave them both my biggest smile.

"Morning girls," Miss Braun said to us.

Miss Crombie furrowed her eyebrows as she focused on me, but she didn't say anything.

Rude, I thought as I carried on walking.

"That's my necklace," I heard Miss Crombie say. "She's wearing *my* necklace."

My eyes widened in alarm, and I touched the necklace. It couldn't be hers, I'd taken it out of Sydney's jewelry box. I turned around and looked over at Sydney, and I saw a knowing glint in her eye.

"Are you sure it's yours?" Miss Braun asked Miss Crombie.

"It was a gift from my Darren, I would recognize it anywhere," she said.

"Harper, what do you have to say about this?" Miss Braun stared sternly at me.

"I, um, I-" I had no idea what to say! I couldn't say I took it from Sydney, could I? So, for one of the few times in my life, I was speechless.

"I found it," I finally spluttered.

"I put it in my office before I went to play tennis," Miss Crombie declared.

"Are you sure you didn't leave it somewhere by accident?" Miss Braun asked her.

"Yes, I'm quite sure."

"I found it at the tennis courts. I was going to hand it in, honestly," I gave my best angelic look. "It's just so beautiful that I wanted to try it on first."

I unfastened the clasp and held it out to Miss Crombie, who glared at me as she took it off me.

"Were you girls behind it too?" Miss Braun looked at Brianna and Taylor.

They stood there silent, not knowing what to say. They could have backed up my story; idiots. Sydney was still watching from further up the corridor. She knew better than to step into the line-of-fire. Instead, she remained a spectator.

"All three of you, my office, NOW!" Miss Braun yelled.

We all trudged our way back up the corridor. "You'll pay for this," I whispered to Sydney, as I passed her.

She smiled at me before she walked off up the corridor. I was left feeling foolish, I knew I'd seen that necklace before, I should have known that it was Miss Crombie's. Sydney was far sneakier than I thought, I definitely needed to watch that girl.

"Sydney," Miss Crombie shouted after her.

I smirked to myself. Finally, she was going to get into trouble too.

"Yes Miss Crombie?" she turned and gave her an innocent look.

"I have a new what's-it-called?" she jabbed her fingers into the air. "A portable phone thingy."

"A cell phone," Sydney said.

"Yes, one of those. Is there any chance you could help me set it up?"

"Sure." Sydney smiled.

Great, I was stuck going to Miss Braun's office while Sydney was being treated like she was little-miss-perfect. She may have won this battle, but she hadn't won the war. I knew what the rest of the initiation rules were, and she was in for a big reality shock.

Chapter Three - Study Time is hell

My necklace prank worked even better than I had envisaged. All three girls ended up with one-week detention, and their parents were notified about their thieving. They also hadn't been through my stuff since and they'd returned everything to me, so all in all, my plan was awesome. I should definitely take up a job as a prank organizer. I'd make a fortune, and then I could move out of home, and not have to deal with mom and her stupid rules again and I could eat an entire tub of Ben & Jerry's while sitting on the couch.

It was study time, and I was sitting at my desk staring at my homework, but not actually doing it. I'd just spent all day in lessons with this bunch of fools, and now I was expected to do a further two-hours of work? I just wanted to watch YouTube videos about far-away beaches, not solve algebra. I couldn't get on the internet though because of this lame school's even lamer no WIFI during study times rule. Like seriously, this was like living in the dark ages.

"Initiation task three." Harper placed a piece of paper down on my desk. "I'd hurry up if I was you, times ticking."

"I'm trying to do my homework," I looked up at her.

"Commit social suicide, see if I care," Harper sniped.

"Fine," I picked up the piece of paper.

There are three tasks, send me the answers, and I'll message you the next task. You have till the end of study time to complete it. If you fail, you will have to forfeit something of my choosing.

"How am I meant to message you the answers when we don't have WIFI?" I raised an eyebrow.

"Not my problem." Harper shrugged.

"But you won't receive them anyway because you don't have WIFI."

"Actually, I will," Harper said smirking.

"How?" I gave her a scrutinizing look.

"I have my ways," she grinned.

Of course, she did. I had presumed that when I saw her on her phone in study hours that she was just reading through her old messages or something. I should have known that rules wouldn't be a barrier for a girl like Harper.

1- *Find out what brand the basketball pole on the court is and message me the answer.*

"How am I meant to do this when we aren't allowed to leave our rooms during study hours?" I asked.

"Not my problem," Harper replied.

"The basketball court is opposite the admin building, someone will see me," I complained.

"Will you just get on with it, you're boring me now." Harper pretended to yawn.

"Beats being stuck with you lot." I stood up.

"This is so exciting." Brianna giggled. "You're going to have a lifetime of detentions if you get caught."

"Or better, you could be expelled." Harper smirked.

"Whatever." I rolled my eyes.

"Good luck," Taylor whispered, as I walked past her.

I left the room and reread the first task. Who cared what brand of pole it was? Seriously, talk about the world's most mundane task. I knew exactly why it was on the list though, the administration office looked over the basketball court. First off, I needed to overcome the WIFI blocking problem. I tried the WIFI on my phone, but it wouldn't connect.

Think, I thought to myself. *Who has a phone with working WIFI, who wouldn't be likely to miss it for a few hours?*

Suddenly Miss Crombie's old face came into my head. Of course, she was totally clueless with technology but better than that, I knew the password for her phone because I'd set it up for her. Now I just had to work out a way to get to her phone. I poked my head around the corner to check that the corridor was empty before I quickly walked over to Miss Crombie's office and knocked on the door.

I was all ready to give her a speech about how I had made a mistake when I set up her phone and needed to borrow it to sort it. I'd tell her that if I didn't fix it, there was a chance it would explode. There was no answer, so I knocked again just to make sure, before I opened the door and crept into her empty office. She'd put it in her desk drawer after I'd helped her set it up, so I checked there…bingo!

I grabbed her phone and slid it into my skirt pocket. Now, I just had to figure out how to get onto the basketball court without being caught. I stood in the corridor and looked out at the court. If I went out there, I'd basically be a sitting duck. There was nowhere to hide, I'd be entirely on show to anyone in the admin building. So, I couldn't just stroll out there and read the pole. I'd have to think of another way of completing the first task.

I chewed on my fingernails as I deliberated what to do. I pulled out Miss Crombie's phone and started to look up popular basketball post brands. I could have guessed, but I didn't want to risk getting it wrong as Harper would be so smug about it. This phone was pretty nifty especially considering that Miss Crombie was about one-hundred-and-eighty years old. I thought I heard a noise behind me, so I jerked on the spot; no one was there. I gave a sigh of relief. I looked down at the phone, I'd accidentally pressed on the camera, and I was staring at myself as it was in selfie mode. It was okay for me, as I looked good but Miss Crombie getting a very accentuated close-up of her wrinkled face wouldn't have been pretty.

I lifted the camera and tilted my head so that I got the best angle. I didn't take any pictures of myself though, I wasn't that stupid. I stared at the zoom button and smiled; of course. I quickly snuck to a window overlooking the court and carefully peaked up from behind the window and aimed the phone at the basketball pole, and then I zoomed in as far as it would go. It was a bit pixelated, and I had to squint, but it was definitely one of the brands that had come up when I'd searched for them.

Harper had jotted down her phone number at the top of the page, so I quickly typed out a message to her and sent it:

Webber Basketball Equipment ;)

I bet Harper was secretly mad that I had completed this task. She'd be putting on a 'not bothered' front to the other girls.

The phone beeped, and task two came through.

The next task isn't so easy. You have to take a photo of the principal's car registration plate.

I rolled my eyes, of course, this was the next task as the staff parking lot was on the other side of the school. I ran along the corridor as quietly as I could and quickly dodged behind a wall when I heard nearby footsteps. They seemed to take ages to go past, which was really annoying. I felt like yelling out, "Like seriously, hurry up, I'm under a time constraint here." I raced through the corridors, and when I reached the other side of the school, I turned on stealth mode.

I used the garden hedge to keep out-of-view by crouching behind it and moving along. My back ached, and I had to hold my nose at one point, so I didn't sneeze, but I reached the end of it and then peered out at the cars. Typically, the principal's car was at the other end of the concrete parking lot and partly disguised by the branches of a willow tree so I couldn't use my zoom-in camera trick this time. Worse than that, a six-foot-high wired fence scaled the perimeter of the parking lot, and there was no hedge to hide behind. I was going to have to make a dash for it.

I looked around me to check that no one else was about, I took a deep breath, and I ran. I spanned the entire length of the wired fenced, dodged behind the tree and then took another deep breath before I leaped out, clicked a picture of the registration number and then darted behind the tree. I leaned against the branch and regained my breath before I sent Harper the picture.

Almost instantly she sent task three through; the final task:

Don't get smug yet, for task three you need to take a snap of the inside of the teacher's staff room.

I reread it and wondered how I was going to complete this one. It's not like I could just stroll in there and casually take a photo. I made my way back to my room without being caught and shoved open the door. All three girls were sitting on Harper's bed, and they all jerked in alarm.

"Oh, it's just you." Harper pulled her phone out from under her pillow. "Are you here to admit defeat?"

"I still have half-an-hour left." I walked over to my desk. "And I'm not a quitter."

"What's her forfeit going to be?" Brianna giggled.

"Now that would be telling." She tapped her nose. "All I'm going to say is that it's a sure-fire way to bring on a social massacre."

Think, I thought to myself, as I tapped my fingers against my desk. *Think!*

How could I sneak into the staff room?

Tap, tap, tap.

"I know you're wetting yourself in fear and all, but quit the tapping," Harper demanded.

I stopped tapping my fingers but not for her benefit, I did it for my own. How could a girl like me get into the staff room? Only I wasn't just any 'girl'…I was the new girl. I picked up my math book and studied the back page of it before I grabbed a pair of scissors out of my desk drawer and made a hole in the back of it that was big enough for the phone camera. I taped the phone securely into place, grabbed the book and then rushed towards the door.

"You only have fifteen-minutes left," Harper shouted after me.

I hurried along the twists and turns of the corridors, whizzed down the stairs and then paused around the corner. I rubbed my eyes until they turned red and then I walked over to the staff room and knocked on the door.

"Yes?" Mrs. Duskel peered down at me, her specs rested on the tip of her nose.

"Is, um, Mr. Dursley in," I gave her my best-concerned look.

I knew full well that Mr. Dursley had already gone home, as in class he was going on about a golf match he was going to.

"Sorry sweetie, he's gone home."

I placed my arm up to my face up as I pretended to burst into tears.

"Sweetie, there's no need for tears. Come in, and I'll get you a glass of water," she beckoned me in.

There were a few other teachers in there, but when they saw my convincing waterworks, they purposely looked the other way. Mrs. Duskel ushered me onto a sunken leather couch before she gave a flustered look as she scanned the room.

"Tissues, tissues, tissues," she muttered under her breath. "Ah, I have some in my handbag. I won't be a minute," she scurried to the other side of the room.

Quickly, I lifted up my math book and snapped a picture of the staff room. With two minutes to go, I sent the picture to Harper.

I closed and then lowered the book just as Mrs. Duskel walked back over to me, she was clutching a packet of tissues in one hand a glass of water in the other. She placed the glass down on the table in front of me and then held the tissues out to me.

"Thanks," I sobbed, as I took them from her.

"So, sweetie, are you going to tell me what's got you so upset?" she awkwardly patted my shoulder.

"I don't understand this math question, and I've been so worried about it. I don't want to get a bad grade."

"Well, I'm no math teacher, but I'm sure I can help you."

"Thank you," I gave her my best fake relieved smile. "It's this question," I opened the book carefully, making sure that she didn't see the hole or phone and then I pointed at the hardest algebra question on the page.

"Oh," she pushed the bridge of her glasses up as she studied the question. "I know this."

"Great," I smiled.

I already knew the answer; of course. Algebra was easy, too easy. She started explaining the answer to me, and I made sure I was smiling as I pretended to listen. Instead, I was thinking about how bummed Harper was going to be that I'd completed her stupid test.

"Thank you," I smiled sweetly at the teacher. "I understand it now."

"Okay sweetie," she followed me across the room. "It's good to see how much your schoolwork matters to you. You're a very promising student."

"School work is extremely important to me," I paused in the doorway. "I was so upset when I got stuck on that question, thank you so much for helping me solve it. I feel much better on everything now."

She gave me a flustered smile and a weird half-wave before she walked back into the staff room. I sneaked back into Mrs. Crombie's office and put her phone back. Not only had I finished Harper's stupidly easy test, but I was now in Mrs. Duskel's good books. The only downside was that she thought I sucked at algebra, even though I was good at it. Oh well, it was totally worth it.

I strutted into my bedroom and fell down onto my bed, a smug look on my face. Harper couldn't mask her annoyance which made my smirk grow wider.

"How did you manage to get into the staff room?" Brianna asked.

"Easy, I made a hole in my textbook, stuck the phone in it and made up some nonsense about being stuck on a math problem."

"That was pretty smart, no one's ever complet…."

"Shut-up Bree," Harper glared at her.

"It was far too easy really, and now Mrs. Duskel thinks I'm a model student," I commented.

"Whatever," Harper muttered under her breath.

I was shocked and fuming, but I was trying really hard not to show Sydney this. No one had ever completed all three tasks before, most of the girls got caught on the first task. In fact, the last girl who'd done it had literally only made it out of the dormitory corridor before Miss Braun caught her and grounded her for the rest of the week.

Sydney wasn't like the other girls, she was smarter than them and sneakier. She didn't let the pressure get to her. She was too determined to just give up.

I looked at her sitting on her bed with an annoyingly smug look on her face, I looked at the red mark on her arm. I knew she had one on her face as well, I'd seen it before she'd covered it up with makeup. So, I did a bit of online snooping and found out some fascinating gossip about our girl Sydney.

Let's just say that rule number four was going to bring her crashing down to reality. It was about time that the other girls saw that she was no match for me.

Chapter Four - Gossip is the word

I'll tell you what rule four is but don't tell Sydney. I want to see the horror on her face when she finds out what it is for herself.

Rule Four- Everyone knows everyone's business. Gossip is traded.

Sydney was in the bathroom, so I used this opportunity to put my plan into action.

"Girls, come here," I gestured them over.

They both stopped what they were doing and hurried over to my bed. Brianna sat down next to me on my bed, but Taylor stood by the side of it looking her usual awkward self.

“Do you wanna hear some gossip about not-so-perfect Sydney?”

“Oooh, tell us.” Brianna’s eyes widened.

“Taylor, what about you?” I looked at her.

“Yeah,” she croaked.

I rolled my eyes, that girl was so lame.

I made a big deal of checking that the coast was clear, and Sydney was nowhere in sight, before I beckoned them closer to me. Brianna shuffled up on my bed, and Taylor leaned further over towards me. I beckoned them in again so that Brianna had shuffled up alongside Taylor and I had no choice but to kneel on my bed.

“Well, you’ve seen that red mark on her arm?”

Brianna gave an enthusiastic nod and then giggled. Taylor just looked awkward, but then that wasn't a shock really.

“She also has one on her cheek that she covers up with makeup. Anyway, they are burn marks.”

“Burn marks?” Brianna sounded shocked. ‘Like from a fire, burn marks?”

Seriously, could this girl get any more stupid? Fire and burn marks tended to go together.

“So apparently, she was so mad with her parents that she started a fire in the kitchen and burnt down her family home.”

“No way!” Brianna stared at me open-mouthed.

"Yes, way. And I think it's only right that everyone knows that we're living with a pyromaniac."

Brianna gave me a confused look, and I rolled my eyes.

"Someone who can't stop themselves from starting fires," I explained.

"Oh!" she giggled.

The bathroom door swung open, and Sydney strode out in school uniform and her wet hair tied up in a towel. We were all staring at her, and it hadn't gone unnoticed.

"I know that you can't help staring at me because I'm so beautiful," she smirked.

"You'd look better without the burn marks," Brianna muttered under her breath.

"What did you just say?" Sydney couldn't hide the alarm in her eyes.

"That your skin looks really glowing today." Brianna giggled before she jumped off my bed and skipped over to hers.

"Oh, okay." Sydney looked away from us and started rummaging through her bedside cabinet.

Now I just needed to sit back and watch my plan unravel. I was about to lie back on my bed when I noticed that Taylor was still kneeling on my bed.

"Get off, you're creasing up my bed cover." I glared at her.

"Sorry." Taylor blushed, as she quickly got off my bed and hurried away.

What a loser she was, then again, they all were. I controlled all of them. I could get them to do whatever I wanted them to do, and they'd do it because I was me and they were them. I was top dog, and they knew it. It was only a matter of time before Sydney knew it too.

"London's burning, London's burning. Fetch the engines, fetch the engines. Fire, fire. Fire, fire," I sang under my breath.

Sydney stopped rummaging. I know that she heard me, after all, I made sure that my singing was loud enough for her to hear. She carried on with what she was doing, but I knew that I'd gotten to her. If only she knew that this was just the beginning.

***

It didn't take long for news of Sydney's pyromaniac past to spread throughout the school. I may have helped it along, but I knew that I could tell a story better than Brianna and Taylor. I told the older girls about it as I collected my breakfast and then I told the group of girls in the restrooms about it, as they did their hair. Hey, they all had a right to know who they were sharing a school with.

Brilliantly, science was our first class of the day. Brianna was sitting next to me on the bench in the old, musky-smelling lab. Sydney was sitting at the back of the room next to a concerned looking Taylor.

Mrs. Dylan didn't seem to notice her unease, probably because she was as old and crumbling as this building was. She was probably only still doing this job because she liked flouncing about in her long, white lab coat.

"We'll be conducting our experiment with the Bunsen burners. Please, can you get into groups of four?" Mrs. Dylan said.

I waved to Tiff and Grace, some of the girls from the room next door, and they joined us without question. I turned around and enjoyed the show, Taylor had joined Amy and Zoe, but they were all staring at Sydney with folded arms and uninviting looks. She stood by their bench trying to look like she wasn't bothered when it was evident to me that she most definitely was.

“You can’t join us,” Amy spat at her.

“We don’t trust you around a flame,” Taylor said.

"Whatever, I'd rather be by myself anyway,” she responded before she sat back down on her seat.

“Sydney, why are you not in a group?” Mrs. Dylan walked over to her.

“I’m not working with *those* girls,” Sydney said.

“Nonsense, go and join them now.”

The other girls in the group all rolled their eyes, but they didn't say anything. Sydney reluctantly walked over to them.

“So, you’re going to find which substances melt, and which burn,” Mrs. Dylan straightened her lab coat. “I suppose you’re an expert on this Sydney?”

The other girls giggled, and Sydney stood there speechless. Mrs. Dylan quickly walked off to another group. I sat there with a smirk on my face, taking delight in the fact that my plan was unraveling even better than I thought it would.

***

I was bored in the cafeteria…yawn! To make it even worse I was stuck with dried up chicken and lumpy potatoes…yuck!

Brianna was going on about her dream boyfriend, Taylor wasn't saying anything because she was a bore and Sydney was sitting there with that stupid confident look on her face. I needed to do something before I died of boredom.

I stood up abruptly and then coughed to clear my voice. The room fell silent, and all eyes were on me.

“I've decided to lighten the mood with a joke,” I shouted. “How do you stop your house from burning down?” There were murmurs and sniggers. I looked down at Sydney, she looked uncomfortable. “Lock Sydney out!” I smirked.

The room erupted into laughter. I sat back down and went back to eating my lumpy mash.

“Good one,” Brianna patted me on the shoulder.

“Yeah, good one,” Taylor said.

Sydney left her barely touched lunch where it was and stormed off across the room. For once she had been unable to think of a good comeback. Rule four had been owned by me and little-miss-not-so-perfect would just have to deal with it.

I continued my victory smirk. Yeah, okay, it was harsh, but this school was my domain, not Sydney's. She was nothing while I was everything.

I was the original wild child, not her. She needed to learn that it wasn't wise to mess with me and that she needed to accept her place in the pecking order. When she did that we'd get along just fine. Until then, she could expect things to worsen for her.

Chapter Five - Locked-Out

So, they knew about the fire, and now everyone was looking at me like I was going to set fire to their bag or something. Apparently, if I were that much of a danger to society, the police would have arrested me. These girls were so naïve and stupid, they let Harper control them, and it was so pathetic. They could taunt me all they wanted, I didn't care. I didn't plan on staying here for much longer, Dad would get through to mom eventually, and I'd join them in New York. I could buy a leopard print faux fur coat from my favorite shop and wear it through Central Park in the winter. This stupid, snotty-nosed school would just be a horrible, brief memory.

Jeez, this place was boring. Study time was over, and I was so bored that I was actually reading a textbook. It beat talking to Harper and her clique though.

"I'm bored," Harper announced.

I rolled my eyes, everyone was bored. This old place took boredom to a whole new level. Trust Harper to make a big deal about it. She was such an attention-seeker, she was so annoying.

"Are you bored too Sydney?" Harper asked.

"Well obviously." I peered at her from above my book. "I'm hardly going to read this otherwise, am I?"

"I thought you were just a dork." She sniggered.

"Do you think nerdy guys are cute?" Brianna asked.

"Not really." I rolled my eyes again.

"This guy from my town likes comics and stuff, but he's quite cute. Maybe he likes me, I've caught him looking at me a few times when he's been pretending to read his comics." Brianna giggled.

"Maybe he just lost his place and looked at you by accident?" Taylor replied.

"Taylor, are you insinuating that no boy could like Bree? That's so mean." Harper couldn't hide her delight.

"No, no, I didn't mean-"

"It sounds to me like you were," Brianna said in a sulky voice.

"No, I wasn't Brianna, honestly." Taylor looked totally flustered.

“It’s okay.” Brianna gave a weak sigh.

I went back to reading my textbook, which was far more exciting than listening to them go on.

“It’s a good job there isn’t a Bunsen burner in here.”

“Yes Harp, fire is my thing.” I rolled my eyes.

Seriously, all I seemed to do at this school was roll my eyes. Also, the fire talk was getting boring now. Besides, the fire had been an accident.

“I say we make it more exciting,” Harper suggested.

“How so?” I gave her a questioning look, as I placed by textbook down on my bed.

“Rule number five,” she said.

Of course, it was going to be another stupid rule.

"Whatever, if it gives me something to do other than being stuck in here looking at your ugly faces, then great."

"Oh, it will!" Harper smirked.

Brianna giggled, and I noticed that Taylor was giving a sly smile. Great, this didn't bode well. Not that I was bothered, these girls couldn't get to me, I was way tougher than they were.

"At this school, your whole life is planned out for you…from the moment you wake up at 6.30am to when the lights go out at 9.30pm. You're told when to eat, when to go to lessons and when to study. The school controls you and turns you into a clone. Don't be a clone Sydney, prove to us that you can fit in here by breaking the school rules."

"So, what are you suggesting, Harper? You want me to creep out of here after lights out and dance around the corridor or something?" I asked.

"I'm sure you can do better than that. We want you to go to the library and check out this book." Harper passed me a folded piece of paper.

"You forget about the locked door," I said.

"It'll be open, I made sure of that," Harper replied.

"Whatever." I snatched the note out of her hand. "I'm only doing this because I'm bored."

"Oh, we believe you Sydney." She sniggered.

I went back over to my bed and picked up my textbook. I pretended to read it, but really, I was thinking about my late-night rule break. The door at the end of the corridor was locked after lights out, so I didn't see how I was going to be able to get to the library. Harper couldn't expect me to evaporate through a solid door so she couldn't fail me for not carrying out an impossible task. Saying that…this was Harper and I knew that she was desperate to see me fail. She was such a horrible person, and I really wanted to see the smirk wiped from her face.

I carried out the normal monotonous routine. I went to dinner, messed about on my phone and then got ready for bed. At 9.30pm it was lights out, and we all hopped into our beds. Mrs. Crombie was on night-time duty, she poked her head around our door to check that we were all in bed. I left enough time for her to check the rest of the rooms and to totter off up the corridor before I pulled my bedcover off me and quietly stepped out of bed. I searched around in the dim light for my shoes.

"Go on then," Harper hissed.

"I'm not doing it barefoot, the floor is gross?" I whispered back.

"Pampered princess."

As if she had the cheek to say that about me. I could have made a smarmy comment back, but I couldn't be bothered. I was going to go and get this stupid book and then come back and go to bed. I slowly opened the door and peered around, there was no sign of Miss Crombie.

"Catch you later, losers," I whispered to the others before I crept out of the room and along the corridor.

I got to the end of the corridor and pushed on the door that was meant to be locked after lights out. Harper had been right. It opened, and I felt my heartbeat increase. Now I had to go to the library to find this stupid book. I sighed before I peered around the door and seeing that it was clear, I hurried down the stairs.

They were stupid girls with stupid challenges. A late-night walk into the library? Like, seriously, was that all they could come up with?

Footsteps shook me from my thoughts and caused me to duck around the corner. I heard whistling and saw heavy black boots pass me. I pressed myself against the wall and tried to control my frantic breathing. I'd heard some of the girls say that there was a security guard, but I hadn't believed them. Why would a snooty school in the middle-of-nowhere need a security guard? This place was more than ridiculous.

I waited until his whistling and footsteps had faded, and then I continued on my walk to the library. This place seemed even eerier at night, it felt like the portrait's eyes were following me as I passed them. The whole school needed to be knocked down and rebuilt, it was seriously freaky. It didn't matter how quietly I stepped, the floorboards still creaked beneath my feet. I bit down on my lip as I carried on walking along the corridor.

I wondered if this place has any ghosts? Not that I was afraid of them, besides there probably wasn't any such thing as ghosts. I reached the library and tried the door; locked. I rolled my eyes. Luckily, I'd come prepared. I took a bobby pin out of my hair and pushed it into the lock. The door to the library was probably as old as Miss Braun, so it was no surprise that it opened with a creak. This was easy, too easy. I stepped into the dusty old library and closed the door behind me. I used my phone light to reread the piece of paper Harper had given to me.

Jane Eyre, Charlotte Bronte, Row 101B

I'd read that book back in one of my former schools, and I hadn't cared for it. Jane was a goody-two-shoes and very dull. Worse still, she married a man who referred to her as 'plain'. There was no way that I would ever marry a guy like that! If a man didn't look at me like I was the most beautiful girl in the world, then there was no chance I would be marrying him. Although I had the added bonus of knowing that I'm incredibly attractive.

I didn't want to linger in the creepy, old library more than I had to, so I tip-toed as quickly as I could over to row 101B and used my phone light to find the book. It had dog-eared edges, and the cover was worn. For the amount they were charging for kids to come to this school, surely, they could have at least bought some new books.

I left the library and managed to dodge the security guard with ease and hurried back to my corridor. I got to the door and went to open it, but it was locked. I told myself not to panic, as I quickly took out my bobby pin and pushed it into the lock. However, this door was more modern, and the bobby pin trick didn't work, no matter how much I tried.

I heard laughter coming from the other side of the door. I knew that it was Harper and the others, this had all been a trick to trap me.

"Let me in." I thudded my fists against the door.

More laughter but they didn't reply, I thudded my fists against the door again, harder this time. My heart was pounding within my chest, and my mouth had gone dry. This was just a joke, they would let me in, they had to let me in!

"Come on, this isn't funny," I banged my fists against the door again.

More laughter was followed by footsteps, and then there was silence.

"Hey, come on," I said, but I knew they'd gone.

Panic set in, what was I going to do now? It was late, and I was locked out. I slumped down onto the floor and leaned my back against the door. I hated this pathetic school, and I hated those nasty girls. This wasn't funny, this was cruel. I stared down at my copy of *Jane Eyre,* the plain looking brown-haired girl on the cover was staring at me, saying...*so what are you going to do now*?

"I hate you," I whispered to her. "I hate you, I hate you, I hate you."

I threw the book onto the floor and then kicked it. It flew across the room, and the pages ruffled before it landed with a thud. Nearby footsteps caused my ears to go into an alert mode. Like a fox, I jumped to my feet, picked up the book and then hurried along the corridor. Whistling, footsteps...the security guard was close by. What a boring, pointless job. Why couldn't they just get alarms like normal places? Talk about being stuck in the dark ages!

I whizzed up the corridor as quickly and quietly as I could. There had to be an open classroom somewhere. I tried some of the classroom doors; locked. I felt too exposed there to use my door opening trick, so I made my way to the next corridor. When I was entirely sure that I couldn't hear any footsteps, I knelt down and went to pull another bobby pin from my hair, only I couldn't find one.

"No, no, no," I whispered. I clenched my hands into fists. My ears twitched, I could hear footsteps. At least I thought I could. I no longer knew if they were real or if they were in my head. Either way, I felt that it wasn't safe to stay around here, so I quickly stood up and hurried along the corridor.

I hate Harper and her stupid friends, they are horrible people. Yes, okay, I hadn't always been perfect, but I'd never been this mean. I circled the school looking for unlocked doors, but I didn't find any. I was so tired, but I had to keep on going, I had to keep on moving away from the security guard.

Seconds, minutes, hours, I don't know how much time had passed precisely, all I know is that time dragged on. I was so tired, I just wanted to curl up in bed and go to sleep. I tried the door near the cafeteria, and it opened. My heart dropped when I saw that it led to a small covered courtyard that was full of large empty cardboard boxes.

My eyelids were drooping, I was so tired. I couldn't keep on wandering around all night. Eventually, I was going to fall asleep in a corridor, and that was a sure-fire way to be caught. I walked over to a box and inspected it before I crawled inside it, closed the flaps and then curled up into a ball. My eyes teared up, but it wasn't because I was sad, it was because I was cold, okay. The box was dark, cramped, uncomfortable and it smelt weird, but my tiredness overwhelmed me, and my dreams took over.

"Excuse me," a voice croaked. "Miss, are you alright?"

I blinked open my eyes and used my arm to shield me from the dawning daylight.

"Huh?" I muttered.

Suddenly the events of last night came back to me, and I jerked upright. I was still out in the courtyard in a box, but someone was standing over me. I looked up at them, my heart pounding. For a horrible moment, I thought it was the security guard, but then I saw the overalls and a concerned smile. It was the janitor, Mr. Meuler.

"Come with me, I'll make you a hot chocolate," he gestured for me to follow him.

I stepped out of the box and stretched out my arms and legs and then I picked up *Jane Eyre*. It was definitely the most uncomfortable place I'd ever slept, but it had been better than wandering around the corridors all night. The sky hadn't fully transitioned into daylight, so I knew that it was early, really early. Still, I looked around cautiously as I followed the janitor along the corridor. The last thing I needed was for Miss Braun to jump out at me and ground me for a month.

He led me into a small, poky room that was full of tools and paints. I sat down on a wooden chair with a wonky leg and watched him as he used the basin in the far corner of the room to fill the kettle up. There was an awkward silence as he waited for it to boil, I contemplated filling the silence, but I was too tired. He poured in some milk and passed me a mug of hot chocolate, and I muttered 'thanks.' Mom never let me drink it back at home, too many calories of course. I blew on it before I took a sip, it was the best tasting drink I'd ever had.

"So," he scratched at his head. "Are you going to tell me why you ended up asleep in one of the boxes?"

I could have made up some elaborate story about how I sleep-walked, it was on the tip of my tongue, but for some reason, I didn't tell him this.

"They locked me out," I blurted. "The other girls, they hate me." I sniffed and tears filled my eyes.

He was silent at first as if he was processing my words. He shuffled towards the door, then stopped and looked back at me.

"Come on." He waved me over. "You'd better be quick if you want to get back before they notice you're missing."

I took another sip of my hot chocolate before I placed the mug down, took the book off my lap and stood up. He waved me over again, and I didn't hesitate this time. I followed him as he weaved his way through the corridors and then stopped in front of the door leading to the corridor that led to my dormitory room. He took a full ring of keys out of his overall pocket and grabbed a middle-sized brass one. He opened the door and then gave me another awkward smile.

"Thanks," I smiled at him.

"My son, he's been bullied too. It isn't nice." He shook his head. "If you need any help, well, then all you've got to do is ask."

"Thank you." I kept my smile.

He gave me a nod, and I quickly walked through the door into the corridor. He closed the door behind me, and I heard him re-lock it. I rushed back to my room, the other girls were all asleep. I could have woken them up and shouted at them, but I didn't. Instead, I crept over to Harper's bed, I saw a mass of white linen and blonde hair. I quietly leaned over and placed *Jane Eyre* down on her bedside table. I walked over to my bed and buried myself beneath the cover. As soon as my head touched the pillow, I gave a relieved sigh. I was safe, at least for now. I wasn't in that cardboard box anymore.

I wondered what mom and dad were up to? Mom was probably at her early morning yoga class and dad was probably on some work trip. Did they ever think about me? Dad would, but I doubted mom gave me much thought. She was probably relieved that I wasn't around anymore, I was a burden to her. I didn't need her, I didn't need either of them.

Harper and her pathetic friends had tried to break me, but they'd failed. I was strong, far stronger than they realized. They could play their little games, but they wouldn't work, I was smarter than they were. I would show them all that I wasn't someone to be messed with. They'd be the last ones laughing when I rose to the top.

Chapter Six - So Magnanimous

The alarm rang throughout the dormitory, and I yawned as I stretched out my arms. That's when I saw something out of the corner of my eye. I sat up, leaned over and grabbed the book that was on my bedside table. I looked at the picture of the pale girl on the front cover; *Jane Eyre.*

I looked over at Sydney's bed, it should have been empty, only there was clearly someone in it bulked up beneath the covers. I couldn't hide my frown, it was far too early for this much disappointment. I wanted to wake up to the news that Sydney had been caught wandering around at night and that she was in significant trouble. I got out of bed and marched over to her bed.

"Morning," I said, as I pulled the cover off her.

She looked startled for a moment and then she looked around the room.

"Morning," she smirked at me. "Are you going to read that?"

I followed her gaze over to my bed where the copy of *Jane Eyre* was. I wanted to know how she'd got back into the room, but I wasn't going to give her the satisfaction of asking her.

"Probably not, it's such a bland book."

"But you do like bland things," Sydney remarked.

I kept my cool even though inside of my head I was screaming. She really thought she was something special, but Sydney needed to realize that she wasn't. I was in charge around here, not her.

She shimmied her way into the bathroom and loudly closed the door. Brianna stirred in her bed.

"W-what time is it?" she opened one eye.

"6.42," I replied with a cranky voice.

Brianna was awful for getting up in the morning, which I found super annoying. It wasn't my job to wake her, she needed to take responsibility for herself, she wasn't a baby.

"Sydney's back," Taylor said in a quiet voice.

Taylor was so quiet and boring that sometimes I forgot that she was there. She was already in her uniform, and she was leaning on her bed against her pumped-up pillows.

“Really?” Brianna giggled. “How?”

“I have absolutely no idea.” Taylor shrugged. “But she came in at 5.17, placed a book on Harper’s bedside table and then got into bed.”

“Loser,” I said under my breath.

I didn't know if I was saying it about Taylor or Sydney. Not that it mattered, as it applied to them both. They were both massive losers and so beneath me.

The bathroom door opened, and Sydney came out wrapped in a towel. Her smugness didn’t hide her tiredness though, the black circles under her eyes were proof of this.

Brianna was now perched on the edge of her bed, her bedcover wrapped around her shoulders.

“How come you didn’t get caught?” Brianna asked.

“Because I’m smart and fast on my feet,” Sydney assertively replied.

“Sorry,” Taylor whispered under her breath.

Sydney rolled her eyes and gave her best ‘not bothered’ look. The girl had style, which I found irritating. She needed bringing back to reality, and I knew just the way to do it. I walked over to her bed and sat down on it.

“Are you here to watch me get dressed?” she asked, raising an eyebrow.

“Hardly,” I sniggered. “It’s time for rule six.”

“Rules, rules, rules, you’re obsessed.” Sydney yawned.

“Aw, is the sad little rich girl frightened?” I tilted my head and stuck out my bottom lip.

“No, I just think your rules are stupid,” Sydney replied.

“Fine,” I stood up abruptly. “Have fun sitting by yourself for the next, um let’s see…forever!!!” I started to walk off.

“Wait,” Sydney called out. “I’ll do it, but only because it gives me something to do.”

“Of course,” I replied before I exchanged a knowing look with Brianna.

I sat down on the edge of my bed and examined my nails. Sydney may have completed rule five, but the next rule was sure to put her in her place.

“Rule six, some teachers are so easy to con, it’s embarrassing, but only *some*. It’s time that you learned which ones to avoid at all costs,” I gloated.

“And how exactly am I meant to do that?” Sydney frowned.

“Oh, I have a way.” I gave a devious smile.

I felt like I'd had about five-seconds of sleep and the more concealer I dabbed under my eyes, the worse the dark circles seemed to look. Still, I'd made it back into the room without getting caught, a fact which was clearly bugging Harper.

Rules, rules, rules, they were all Harper babbled on about. Boring, they were so incredibility boring. Yawn! But like, whatever. I wasn't one to back down to a challenge, so I'd complete her stupid rules just to shut her up.

I was sitting opposite Harper in the cafeteria and trying my best not to face-plant into my lumpy porridge. She looked smug, too smug. She apparently had something on her mind, I wanted her to just come out with it now so that I could get on with my day. In fact, I just wanted today to be over with! I desperately needed to sleep.

"So, are you ready to hear your next task?" Harper stirred her spoon around her bowl of soggy cornflakes. "Or are you chickening out?"

"Go on," I raised my chin trying to look confident and smug.

"So, this task is all about finding out which teachers are easy to wrap around your little finger." Harper stuck out her pinkie. "And which are not."

On hearing this, Brianna giggled, and Taylor gave an uneasy look.

"You have to ask each teacher in front of the class if zebras are black with white stripes or white with black?" Harper commanded.

Brianna giggled again. She was like one of those annoying toys that made sounds when you pressed its tummy but then didn't shut up for ages. It was a shame that I couldn't switch her off by taking her batteries out.

"Also, you have to use the word 'magnanimous' when you're talking to the teacher."

"Okay," I tried to maintain my unfazed look.

"You have no idea what it means do you?" Harper smirked.

"Of course, I do," I protested.

"Right, what does it mean then?"

"It's not my problem that you don't know what it means, you should take your moronic friends and look it up," I hissed.

"Whatever." Harper grinned. "Come on, we've got a class to get too." She stood up, and her 'friends' followed her.

I sat at the back of the English classroom next to Ruby, she was totally annoying at times and fiddled with her wild red hair way too much, but it was good to have a break from Giggles, and Mouse. Our teacher, Mr. Watson had a bright pink sweater on, and he was walking up and down the aisle with his hand in his pocket while he went on about some boring book from the dark ages.

"Sir," Sydney stuck her hand up into the air.

Let the fun begin, I thought to myself.

"Yes," he spun on the spot and looked at her. "What can I do for you young Sydney?"

"Well, I was just wondering if zebras were black with white stripes, or white with black?"

"Interesting," he brought his hand up to his chin and rested it there. "Very interesting. What a conundrum. Five merit points for thinking outside of the square and for posing a question that reflects one of the many fascinating quandaries of life."

Quandaries of life, trust Mr. Watson to come out with such nonsense. Most of the class were laughing, but he didn't seem to mind this. Apparently, he was a writer in his spare time and had been published in some prestigious prose magazine. Writers were clearly all bonkers!

"Thank you, sir, that is very magnanimous of you," Sydney said with a huge smile on her face.

"Such extraordinary use of vocabulary, five more merit points for you."

"Thanks, sir," Sydney replied.

Everyone else sniggered but I rolled my eyes, Mr. Watson was such an idiot. This was an easy start for Sydney but not every teacher here was as soft as Mr. Watson.

The next class was history, Miss Alanke was a teacher who had a somewhat sour disposition. I'm sure that she thoroughly dislikes all children and hates her job.

"Miss, I was pondering something and wondered if you could help me?" Sydney shouted out.

"In this class, you put your hand up when you want to ask something, and then you wait to be addressed," she snapped back at Sydney.

"Erm, okay, so, I was wondering, are zebra black with white stripes, or white with black stripes?" Sydney asked.

"Stop trying to disrupt my class with silly comments, that has just earned you a detention."

"What? That's so magnanimous of you," Sydney replied.

"Make that two detentions!" Miss Alanke shouted.

The rest of the girls giggled, including me. This was hilarious, thank goodness for Miss Alanke!

Next up was the cooking class, and the lost-in-the-clouds, Ms. Ekelby. She once made a cake with salt instead of sugar and offered it out to the rest of the staff.

Sydney sat near the front of the class, on a bench next to Brianna. We were making cupcakes, which I guess was better than math class, but still, it seemed pretty pointless to me. My parents weren't paying a small fortune for me to learn how to make cupcakes.

"Miss, so I need to cook them magnanimously for twenty

minutes?" Sydney asked.

"Urm…" Ms. Ekelby looked confused. "Twenty-minutes, yes."

I sniggered to myself, she was as clueless about the word as Sydney was.

"Miss, do you think that zebras are black with white stripes or white with black stripes?" Sydney asked.

"Are you okay, Sydney," Ms. Ekelby asked before she walked over to the next workbench and started talking to the girls there.

I had to bite down on my bottom lip to stop myself from laughing-out-loud. Okay, so Sydney might not have received any more detentions, but the teacher's reaction was priceless. She obviously thought that Sydney was strange, really strange!

The last class of the day was geography, and I was hopeful that this would go brilliantly…well, for onlookers but definitely not so much for Sydney. Mr. Thompson was an old-school teacher, he was ancient for a start, and I'd heard a rumor that he and Miss Braun were having a secret affair…yuck! He always stood and moved really stiffly, he always wore an undersized suit, and if anyone so much as coughed out of place, he always knew the source of the disruption and punished them for it. Even I had received detentions from Mr. Thompson, and my sweet-talking only ever made it worse. He wasn't an average person, he was some form of an emotionless robot.

"What can you tell me about the magma chamber of a volcano?" he asked the class.

Immediately several kids shot their arms up into the air,

including Sydney. Only she didn't wait for him to ask her to answer.

"It's where the lava is formed before it is released through the vent, that's so magnanimous," Sydney smiled.

"Firstly, I advise you not to speak unless you've been spoken to," he stared at her. "Secondly I expect you to write me three paragraphs where you use the word magnanimous correctly."

The class sniggered including me. Mr. Thompson's eyes darted from one-kid-to-the-next.

"Silence," he said sternly.

"Sir," Sydney shouted out. "Do you think that zebras are black with white stripes or white with black?"

Mr. Thompson turned an angry shade of red and the vein on his neck pulsed.

"I will not tolerate fools in my classroom. Get out!" he shouted, as he pointed at the door.

There were murmured sniggers and giggles as Sydney gathered up her books and walked across the room. As she passed me, she smiled, and I found myself doing the same back. It was evident that Mr. Thompson was definitely not magnanimous.

Still, I had to admit that I was impressed with the new girl's guts, she was definitely no coward, not even when it came to Mr. Thompson, and most of the girls here were terrified of him. No one had ever done as well on this rule before, most of the time the new girls asked a silly question, got into trouble and then kept their mouths closed after that.

This Sydney girl wasn't like the others. She was definitely one to watch!

Chapter Seven - No Boys Allowed

So okay, I ended up with a week's worth of detentions and some lines, but it was totally worth it, just to show Harper that I wasn't afraid. It was also kind of funny, especially Mr. Thompson's reaction. That man needed to lighten up, he should seriously consider therapy.

Another day meant, of course, another rule. This time Harper told me when we were studying in the library. "Rule seven, contact with boys is not allowed; apparently," she whispered.

Really, did we have to do this here of all places? I could feel the aged librarian's eyes boring into me.

"You have to sneak out and get a selfie with a boy our age," Harper whispered.

"How am I meant to do that?" I hissed back.

"Shush." Harper smiled and looked at her book. The librarian was staring at both of us.

As soon as she moved away, I mouthed to Harper, "How?"

"Shush!" The librarian shot me a dirty look. She was very sneaky, it was like she had naughty girl radar attached to her ears.

Harper shrugged before she turned her attention back to her studying.

I was stuck in an antique building in the middle-of-nowhere, how was I meant to get a selfie with a boy? This played on my mind for the rest of my study time. I was contemplating photoshopping a picture of me with a boy, but then I went back to my room and found a plastic red rose on my pillow. There was a scribbled note next to it:

Make the boy hold this so that we know he's real.

Great, there goes my photoshop plan. I chewed on my nails as I thought about how I could complete this task. Suddenly, Mr. Meuler came into my head, he had said to ask him if I needed help and he had a son around my age. Hopefully, he'd be helping his dad out today, now all I needed to do was to find the janitor.

I rushed out of the room and started to whizz around the school grounds. I checked Mr. Meuler's workroom first but he wasn't there, so I went from room-to-room looking for him. Eventually, I found him polishing the floor of the gymnasium, only he wasn't alone, his son was there too.

I hurried over to Mr. Meuler and gave him my best needy smile.

"Hi Sydney, how's everything going?" he asked.

"The girls are hassling me again. They want me to give this to a boy," I held up the flower.

"I can get you a real one if you'd like? I doubt Elliot would be really impressed with that, it's wilting, and it's not even real," Mr. Meuler chuckled.

"It has to be this one, I need a picture of us together, and he has to be holding it." The words had rushed out of my mouth, I sounded desperate.

"Ah, okay," he replied, scratching his head. "Elliot." He waved his son over.

Okay, so he was cute, even cuter than I remembered. I liked his floppy brown hair and intense eyes.

"You remember Sydney?" He pointed to me.

"Um, yeah." he gave an awkward smile.

"Hey," I said, smiling back at him.

"Sydney is being hassled by some of the girls. I found her locked out of her corridor the other night. Anyway, she needs you to hold this rose and be in a picture with her, then hopefully the other girls will stop bothering her. You know what it's like to be bullied, it's not good, not good at all." He shook his head.

"Um, okay." Elliot gave a puzzled and embarrassed look. "What do you want me to do?" he asked.

"Please hold this." I passed him the flower.

He took it from me and held it out awkwardly. I stood next to him and aimed my camera at us, but I couldn't get a good shot. I moved in closer to him, and my arm brushed against his. Then Mr. Meuler came to the rescue and offered to take the photo.

"Smile," he called out.

I gave my best smug look into the camera.

Elliot gave an awkward smile which I had to admit looked cute, and I took a couple of pictures.

"Thanks." I smiled at Elliot. I wanted to tell him how totally grateful I was, but 'thanks' was the only word that managed to escape my lips.

"No problem." Elliot held the flower out awkwardly.

I took it from him, and we exchanged embarrassed looks. I looked through the pictures and sent the best one to Harper with a red heart and red rose emojis beneath it.

“Thanks,” I said again. Now I really sounded lame.

“No problem, I’ll probably see you around.” He smiled, and his whole face lit up. Unfortunately, so did my face…I had turned bright red.

“I hope so,” I replied before I hurried off across the gymnasium.

“Thank you!” I waved over at Mr. Meuler as I passed him.

“Bye Sydney.” He waved back.

***

"I suppose he's a bit cute," Harper was sat cross-legged on her bed studying the picture. "I mean, from certain angles."

"I think he's adorable," Brianna squealed, as she looked over Harper's shoulder. "Where did you find him?"

"Somewhere," I gave a sly smile.

"He's not my type, but he could be worse looking, I guess," Harper shrugged.

"You already said that he's cute," Taylor corrected her.

"Remind me how you did on this task, Taylor?" Harper glared at her. "Oh yeah, you failed!"

Taylor blushed as she hurried over to her bed. I wondered if one day Taylor would receive one dig too many, and she'd blow up at Harper, or if she never would? She probably never would which was kind of a shame, it would have been amusing to watch.

"Is he your boyfriend now?" Brianna asked me.

"No," I shook my head. "I barely know him."

"He's cute though, you two look great together."

"Well, I suppose." I flicked my hair behind my back.

I heard Harper snigger, but I ignored her. I knew that she was secretly fuming that I'd found a cute boy to pose in a picture with me. Elliot was sweet, and he'd been lovely helping me out. He was even more attractive than this boy called Charlie back at my old school. Hopefully, he had better taste than him too, as Charlie chose this super plain, goody-two-shoes girl called Remmy.

I got into bed and closed my eyes. Elliot was such a cool name, and he was so cute, awkwardly so, which somehow made him even sweeter. Maybe this decrepit school wasn't so bad after all?

Chapter Eight - Roomie Besties

At boarding school, it helps a lot if you can get on with your roommates. Imagine sharing a room with someone you hated? Yeah, not great. The important thing was that I didn't actually hate anyone, if I did, then there was no way that I would continue sharing a room with them. I didn't hate giggly Brianna, even though she got on my nerves. I didn't hate Taylor, even though she was utterly dull most of the time. I didn't even hate the new girl, I actually found tormenting her amusing. She didn't cower and give up as quickly as the other girls did. This didn't change the fact that she needed to realize that when it came to this bedroom, I was in charge just like I was with everything else.

When I told a lame joke, Brianna and Taylor laughed as though I was funnier than James Corden. When I asked Brianna to do my math homework for me, she didn't hesitate (even though she answered half of the questions wrong and I had to redo them.) When I asked Taylor to grab something for me, she did. They were under my spell, I just needed to figure out a way to break Sydney, so that I had her under my control too.

It was a typical boring Saturday afternoon, Miss Crombie had taken Sydney on a tour of the school, so I decided to have some fun. Brianna was sitting on her bed with her headphones in and Taylor was sitting at her desk drawing.

"Brianna," I shouted. "Brianna," I waved my arms in front of her.

She pulled out one of the earphones and looked at me.

"I want you to go to the art room and get some cellophane," I ordered her.

"Okay Harper," she jumped off her bed and walked towards the door. "Why?" She looked back at me.

"I want to play a trick on little-miss-perfect," I smirked.

I watched the look of realization appear on Brianna's face when she eventually figured it out.

"Oh, okay." She giggled before she hurried off.

I looked over at Taylor, she was lost to her drawing. I could have left her be, but where was the fun in that? These girls needed to know their place in the pecking order.

"Taylor!" I shouted.

I watched with glee as she snapped out of her trance.

"Yes?" she looked at me.

"Take Sydney's mattress cover off and her pillowcase," I ordered.

Taylor put down her pencil and obediently walked over to Sydney's bed and did as I asked. I smirked to myself, having all the power was great.

Brianna reappeared with a roll of cellophane under her arm.

"Great, now put it on her bed and pillow."

They both did as I asked, then they put the mattress sheet and pillowcase back on. I opened the drawer on my bedside table and rummaged around in it. I pulled out my trusty plastic spider and held it in my palm so the other girls could see it.

Brianna squealed and hid behind Taylor.

"It's obviously not real." I rolled my eyes.

"Oh," Brianna giggled.

"It's the finishing touch to my plan," I walked over to Sydney's bed and buried the spider underneath her bedcover.

I rubbed my hands together, there was no better feeling than setting up a good plan.

An hour later Sydney returned. None of us so much as looked at her as she flounced into the room.

"That was so boring," she walked over to her desk and started rummaging through the draw. "And then Miss Crombie made me drink tea in her office and went on and on about tennis."

I carried on looking at my phone and ignored her. The others did too, although Brianna was giggling softly to herself. That girl seemed incapable of silence.

"Whatever," Sydney said. She pulled her headphones out of the draw. "You girls are boring me, so I'm going for a walk."

I didn't look up as she left, and I hid my smirk behind my phone. As soon as the door closed behind her, Brianna burst into laughter, and we all exchanged knowing looks.

The rest of the day passed by in a ball of boredom. Okay, so at least there aren't any classes on a Saturday afternoon, but there's little else to do. I didn't want to watch the awful black and white movie that was playing in the gymnasium or play bingo with Miss Crombie in the main hall. I mostly hung out in my room listening to music, scrolling through my phone and making sure that no one spoke to Sydney.

By the time the bell rang for lights out, I could tell that the silence was getting to Sydney. Taylor hopped out of her bed and switched off the light. Sydney sat down on her bed *crinkle, crinkle, crinkle*. We all quietly giggled, but Sydney didn't make a comment.

"Goodnight Brianna," I said.

"Goodnight Harper," she giggled back.

"Goodnight Taylor," I called out.

"Goodnight Harper," Taylor replied.

"Goodnight Taylor." Brianna giggled.

"Goodnight Brianna," she replied.

"Night girls." Sydney tried to join in.

We all ignored her.

She got into bed, crinkle, *crinkle, crinkle.* She placed her head on the pillow, and the ruffling sounds were even louder.

Our muffled laughter escaped from beneath our bedcovers, this was hilarious.

I was expecting her to go into a meltdown, rip the covers off and freak out. She didn't do this. Instead, she stayed in her bed and purposely moved around so that it made even more noise. I buried myself further under the cover and placed my hands over my ears. After twenty-minutes of Sydney tossing-and-turning, I couldn't take it anymore, the crinkling noise was excruciating.

I jumped out of bed, marched over to Sydney and pulled her cover off. She was lying there with her eyes closed and her expensive looking headphones on. I yanked them off her, and she looked at me with an eyebrow raised.

"Get up!" I ordered her.

"What's wrong Harper, you look upset?" Sydney feigned concern.

"Stand up!"

This time Sydney ignored me and closed her eyes, I grabbed her arm and pulled at it. She tried to shake me off, but I kept on pulling. It wasn't long before Brianna and Taylor appeared and helped me drag her off the bed. She slid onto the floor with a groan, and I immediately took the mattress cover off and ripped off the cellophane. I did the same with the pillow, and then I turned around to see that Sydney was standing there, her hands were on her hips, and even in the near-darkness, I could see the smirk on her face.

"No more noise!" I grunted before I went back over to my bed and got into it.

Silence descended, quiet, glorious silence.

I awoke to a deafening scream. Someone switched the light on, and I instantly covered my eyes. I sat up and blinked open my eyes, then I saw that Sydney was up and pointing at something on her bed.

"S-spider!" She sounded terrified.

I got out of my bed and walked over to Sydney's. I picked up the plastic spider and held it as if it was real. Sydney looked horrified, and she jumped backward, bashing her foot on her desk.

"Ouch!" she screamed.

I sniggered. "Sydney, what have you got against Gordon, he just wants to say hello." I held my hand, which had the spider in it, out to her.

"Go away!" she dodged under my arm and whizzed off across the room and ran straight into Mrs. Crombie.

"Girls, what is all this racket about?" She glared at a startled looking Sydney.

"Harper set her pet spider on me, and it's huge. I just want to sleep miss, but I'm not sharing a room with a spider," Sydney wailed.

While Sydney was talking, I quickly slipped the plastic spider into the back of my undies.

"I don't have a pet spider Miss, I think Sydney must have had a nightmare." I gave Mrs. Crombie an innocent look.

"Yeah, as if Harper would have a pet spider." Brianna giggled.

"Yeah, that's crazy," Taylor added.

“She does, it’s in her hand.” Sydney pointed.

I opened both of my empty hands and then shook my head.

“Miss, please can you send Sydney to another room? We're trying to sleep, and she's keeping us awake with her ridiculous stories,” I asked.

“No one is moving rooms. Harper, you need to have more patience with Sydney, she’s new here.” She gave me a dirty look.

“We have been nothing but kind and caring towards Sydney, we are model roommates.” I managed not to laugh.

“I’m glad to hear it,” replied Miss Crombie.

Most of the teachers liked me here, but Mrs. Crombie didn't, and she liked me even less after the jewelry incident. It was a shame Miss Alkane didn't do night duties, as she probably would have made Sydney sleep in the corridor. Mrs. Crombie searched Sydney's bed.

“All good.” she smiled and gestured for Sydney to go back to her bed.

“Thank you,” Sydney replied.

“Now go to sleep, I’ll stay here until you all have.”

Sydney got back into bed, and Mrs. Crombie turned the light off and then sat down on Taylor's desk chair.

Oh well, at least I'd freaked Sydney out, and now she thought I had a pet spider, which was amusing. All-in-all it'd been a good prank.

No one made a fool of me and got away with it, it was definitely payback time. I put my plan into action the following night. I waited until I was sure that the other girls were asleep, then I crept over to Harper's bed. She had one arm out of the cover; perfect. I used a soft point pen to draw a black dot on her forearm. I tip-toed back over to my bed, a devious grin on my face.

The next morning, I sat on my bed, and as soon as I saw Brianna walk out of the bathroom, I stretched out my arms.

"Hey Brianna, how long are your arms?" I asked.

Brianna sat down next to me and stretched out her arms so

that we could compare, my arm was longer than hers.

Harper came over to us, she plonked herself down next to Brianna and stretched out her arms. That girl is so competitive, I knew she wouldn't be able to resist.

"Mine is the longest." Harper gave a satisfied grin.

"What's that?" Brianna pointed at the black dot.

Harper examined it with a horrified expression. She tried rubbing it off, but I'd used a permanent marker, so it didn't fade.

"It's nothing." She quickly stood up and walked away.

I caught her glancing at it a few times, and I had to try really hard to hide my smirk.

***

That night, I crept over to Harper's bed and made the mark slightly bigger. Both Brianna and Taylor commented on it the next morning.

The following night, I make the dot slightly bigger, and this time I added a smaller dot just above the first. The next morning Harper looked at her arm with concern, Brianna and Taylor tried to reassure her that it was nothing but Brianna's worried giggles and the fact that Taylor stayed at least three feet away from Harper told another story.

In the cafeteria, several girls surrounded Harper and inspected the mark.

"You could have the lurgy," Ruby said.

"What's the lurgy?" Brianna asked, giggling.

"She could be infectious," Ruby added with some authority

to her voice.

Brianna instantly pushed her tray away from Harper and shuffled up the bench.

"It's nothing, okay," Harper snapped.

"Go to the nurse," Amy suggested.

"Yeah Harper, I really think you should go to the nurse," Meg remarked. "If it is contagious, you could infect the whole school."

A couple of the girls immediately placed their hands over their mouths and noses. I noticed that Harper's eyes were tearing up, it turns out that she wasn't as hard as she thought she was.

"I'm not contagious!" Harper abruptly stood up, then stormed off out of the cafeteria.

Brianna shrugged her shoulders before she hurried after her.

"Maybe it's the plague," Amy said.

"What if Harper turns into a zombie and tries to eat our brains?" Zoe added.

"I highly doubt it's that." Taylor couldn't hide the worry from her voice.

I sat there in silence and ate my breakfast. I didn't need to say or do anything else, my plan was working fabulously. I was relishing sitting back and watching it unravel.

After about ten-minutes, Harper and Brianna returned. Harper looked unimpressed, and Brianna was trying really hard not to laugh.

"What is it, Harper?" Taylor asked. "It's not serious is it?"

“No,” she shook her head. “They were pen marks,” she whispered.

“Huh?” Taylor asked.

“They were pen marks.”

The other girls overheard and burst out laughing. I noticed how red Harper’s cheeks had gone and I fed off her embarrassment. I didn't join in with the laughter though. Instead, I gave her a sly smile.

“The nurse wiped them off with a swab,” Brianna giggled. “Then she got so mad at Harper for wasting her time that she gave her a detention.”

The rest of the girls laughed, and Harper sat there with her arms folded, looking furious.

“I know this was you,” she snarled at me. “I won’t forget.”

She rushed out of the cafeteria and Brianna ran after her.

“What does she mean?” Zoe asked me.

“Beats me.” I shrugged before I shoveled a spoonful of porridge into my mouth.

Chapter Nine - Sneak-Out

It was Sunday morning, but instead of being allowed one lie-in in this lousy place, I had to get up early for church. I mean seriously, how ridiculous was that? No one should be forced to go to church, I should have freedom of choice. Worse still, we had to walk twenty minutes up the road to reach the local church, and we had to wear our school uniforms.

On the walk there, I purposely lingered near the back. Harper and her gang were ahead of me, and I had no intention of joining them. They'd made me look dumb in front of Miss Crombie with their stupid spider trick. So okay, Miss Crombie took my side, but it was still super creepy. At least I got one over on them with their cellophane trick, my trusty headphones did the job there.

The girls from the room next to me stopped walking and

waved at me. I didn't know that much about them, besides their names. I smiled as I reached them, and they walked alongside me.

"Hi Sydney," Tiff said.

"Hey."

"School life is so boring." Tiff yawned.

"Yeah, we need some excitement," Grace added.

"After church, we're going to go into town, are you coming?" Tiff smiled at me.

"Are we allowed to do that?" I asked

"Of course not," she chuckled. "We're sneaking out."

"You should come with us," Grace said.

I paused to think about it. This could be a Harper set-up, but that girl wasn't in charge of everything and everyone, I was probably just being paranoid. They seemed genuinely friendly and why wouldn't they want to include me in their group? After all, I was always in huge demand at my previous schools.

"Yes, I'll come," I replied. Feeling happy for the first time since I came to this school.

"Great!" Tiff grinned. "You'll only need $10 which will cover your bus ticket and food. Meet us in the gymnasium an hour after the church service finishes."

"Okay," I smiled.

"Great, see you then." All three girls smiled and waved at me as they walked off. It would be good to escape for a while, and those girls seemed cool. However, there was an uneasy feeling in my gut, but I chose to ignore it.

Sneaking out, what could possibly go wrong? I thought to myself.

***

I walked into the gymnasium to see the other three girls waiting for me. We had all changed out of our uniforms and into our own clothes, and everyone looked excited at the prospect of leaving this stifling old place.

"Hey Sydney, glad you made it." Tiff smiled.

I smiled back. I didn't know how they planned on sneaking out of here, but they must have had a plan. Grace positioned herself by the gymnasium door as a lookout, and I followed the others into the store cupboard. Tiff went over to the window and pushed it open.

"Success!" She grinned.

Hannah rushed out and returned with Grace. We all climbed through the window which led onto the visitors' car park, and we sneaked past the few cars in the carpark, through the open gate and ran off around the corner. They stopped to catch their breath and then giggled excitedly.

"What happens if the gate gets locked?" I asked.

"Don't worry, our friend has the key. If it's locked, we'll message her to come and open it," Hannah said.

This made me feel a bit better, but still, the uneasy feeling in my gut remained. We walked down to the bus stop, bought tickets from the machine and hopped onto the bus. Then we all gave our tickets to Tiff to look after, as she had a backpack. I thought that this was sweet of her, they all seemed nice and friendly.

We chatted away on the bus journey, and I looked out of the window and watched as the small mall came into view. It wasn't quite Venice Beach standards, but it would do. We hopped off the bus and hurried into the mall. It felt so good to be out of school, I finally felt like I could breathe.

"Oooh, that dress would look so nice on you," Tiff pointed at a lilac sun-dress that was on a mannequin in one of the shop windows. "It would look amazing against your skin tone."

"Yeah, it's pretty," I smiled.

"You're beautiful, Sydney," Grace said, as she swept some of her ash-blonde hair behind her back.

"Yeah, so pretty," Tiff agreed.

"Thanks." I blushed. It felt so good to know that these girls liked and admired me. My self-confidence had taken a bit of a dive since I came to boarding school.

"Let's go and get some food, I'm so hungry," Tiff suggested.

The other girls agreed, I glanced back at the dress before I followed them.

We went into a fast food restaurant, and we all ordered a mini pizza and a large coke. Mom would have freaked out if she'd seen what I was eating, that would have bothered her far more than the fact that I'd sneaked out.

We spent the next hour looking around the shops and trying on oversized hats and glitter-framed sunglasses. Tiff announced that we had better get back to school, so we started to head out of the mall, as we reached the shop with the lilac dress in the window, she stopped.

"Sydney, I think you should try that dress on." she placed

her hands on her slim waist.

"But we'll miss the bus," I replied.

"There's loads of time." She pulled her backpack down and rummaged in the front pocket. "You two go ahead, I'll wait with Sydney," she passed Grace and Hannah their tickets.

As they walked off to the bus stop, I followed Tiff into the shop. She rushed over to the rail with the lilac dresses on and pulled out my size.

"Perfect!" She held it against me. "Go and try it on."

"But I don't have the money for it anyway." I blushed.

"Doesn't mean you can't try it on. You could always buy it next time." Tiff sounded so enthusiastic that I couldn't say no.

I gave a nod before I took the dress from her and hurried over to the changing rooms. I tried it on and examined myself in the mirror, it was gorgeous. I wondered if Elliot would think I looked good in it? Of course, he'd think that. I looked good in everything. I pulled open the curtain.

"What do you think?" I said, only no one was there. I walked out into the store and searched around for Tiff, but I couldn't find her. The uneasy feeling in my gut intensified. I rushed back into the changing room and changed out of the dress, and then I rushed to the bus stop. There was no sign of the bus or the girls. I tried to calm myself down and told myself I could just get the next bus, but then the realization hit me that Tiff had my ticket and I didn't have any money for a new one.

I sat down at the bus stop and thought through what to do. Fifteen minutes later the bus arrived, I rubbed my eyes and started to sniff, and then I stepped onto the bus and walked up to the bus driver.

"Ticket please," he muttered to me.

"I-I had it," I did my best fake sobbing, "It was in my pocket, but now it's gone, and I don't have any more money, and I won't be able to get home, and I don't know what to do."

"Calm down miss." He gave me an uneasy look.

"And I forgot my phone, so I can't ring anyone, and I don't know what to do."

"Go on," he pointed up the aisle of the bus. "Just don't tell anyone or they'll think I'm too soft." He gave me a sympathetic smile.

"Thank you, thank you so much." I darted up the aisle and sat by the window.

How dare those girls trick me like that. Why was I so stupid? I sighed to myself as I slumped further down in my seat. I should have known that Harper had set them up, those girls had barely acknowledged me before today.

I got off the bus and walked back to school. I gave a sigh of relief when I saw that the side gate was open. I was about to walk through it when I saw Mrs. Crombie standing in the car park, talking to some parents.

A mom and her daughter walked through the car park, they had apparently been on an approved visit. I contemplated joining them but decided against it, I would have stuck out. Instead, I waited it out until a larger group of parents, a grandmother, two girls around my age and a younger girl all walked up to the school entrance. *Perfect*, I thought, as I quickly walked up behind them. The younger kid was struggling to carry her shopping bags.

"Need a hand?" I smiled at her.

She gave me a smile, so I took one from her.

"I had such a good day shopping, I bought this cute dog plushie and a sparkly print skirt," she said.

"Sounds great." I kept my smile.

Mrs. Crombie was so busy talking to the parents that she didn't notice me pass her. When we got into the school grounds, I gave the bag back to the girl, said "bye" and waved at her as I hurried off to my dorm. Harper was standing in the corridor talking to Tiff, Grace, and Hannah, and when they saw me, their faces dropped.

"Hey girls," I walked up to them. "I decided to leave the dress, it looked a bit cheap. Thanks though, I had a great day," I gave my best fake smile.

I walked off into my room, slumped down onto my bed and gave a massive sigh of relief.

Harper

As much as it pained me to say it Sydney had passed rule nine- *weekends are boring, learning how to sneak out will save you.*

Sydney was strong-minded, determined, stubborn and quick-thinking. I didn't overly like her, but I did respect her. I held the verdict meeting in my room and loads of girls came, far more than usual. They all squashed in and sat on the beds, the floor, wherever they could find a space.

"So, as you know, all new girls have to partake in the nine-rule initiation test to see if they are worthy of acceptance here. Sydney is a pain, a massive one at that, but she did well, and for that reason, she has passed." I looked over at Sydney and smirked.

The room erupted, and the girls cheered and congratulated Sydney.

"Thank you," Sydney addressed the crowd. "And thank you, Harper, for setting the challenge, I had so much fun."

We exchanged knowing looks with each other. The girls flocked over to her to suck-up to her and congratulate her some more. I turned my attention back to my group where Brianna was going on about boys as usual.

Sydney may have passed the test, but she's no match for me. After all, I am the original wild child, and I rule this school.

Book 2

Harper + Sydney
= TROUBLE

Chapter One - Friend or Foe

When it came to the new girl, Sydney, it seemed that I had a choice. I could either try to break her spirit or be her friend. I deliberated this in my favorite place in this school, which was the overgrown garden area on the other side of the largest of the perfectly kept lawns. It was hidden behind several thick oak trees, so I presumed that most people didn't realize it existed and that the gardeners didn't bother with it for this reason. I liked it here, it was silent, private and mine, all mine. I took a chocolate bar that I'd snatched off one of the younger kids out of my pocket and undid the wrapper. It was a humid day, so the chocolate had melted onto the foil. I took a bite and then licked my chocolaty fingers.

Sydney, Sydney, Sydney - friend or foe?

Reasons why I should be her friend...

We shared a room so surely getting along with the girl would make life easier? Surely it would make her stop the pranks? As much as it pained me to admit it, she was smart and good at fooling people. I mean, she wasn't at my level of a genius prankster, but she was annoyingly good at them. She always seemed one step ahead of everyone and everything (apart from me of course.) She'd passed my rule test, and I'd designed that to be hard. I was friends with Brianna and Taylor, and they were both pretty stupid, maybe having a smart friend wasn't a bad thing.

I could try and break Sydney down and make her feel like her life wasn't worth living, but the girl was already stuck in this awful school. Also, her parents seemed to totally suck. They hadn't visited her once, and I'd never heard her on the phone to them. Brianna called her mom every night and Taylor got a call from her parents on weekends, but Sydney's parents never checked in on her. Maybe behind those pretty eyes of hers was a world of pain. Did I want to add to that? Nah, not really.

Reasons why I should be her enemy...

She was cunning, I never knew what was going on in that head of hers, and that unnerved me. I was the smart one, I was in charge. Girls way older than me did my bidding because they knew that it made sense to have me on their side. I'd never met anyone that was as devious as me, and I didn't know how to take this. Still, I could have broken her, I was sure of that. I could have made sure that none of the girls spoke to her. I could have smashed eggs in her bed and rubbed stinging nettles onto her school uniform, but wouldn't this just start a war? Yes, I would have won because I had everyone on my side and she had no one, but I knew that she wouldn't have gone down without a serious fight. Then what? She would be expelled or leave or whatever, where would she go? This school was lame, but as boarding schools went I kind of liked it (Shush! Don't tell anyone I said that.) So yeah, seeing Sydney squirm would have made me smile, but was it worth the effort?

Friend or foe, friend or foe? Decisions, decisions. Naturally, it was down to me, the power was in my hands. I leaned back against one of the trees, finished off my chocolate bar, stuffed the sticky wrapper into my pocket and then wiped my fingers on a leaf. I noticed a pile of nettles in front of me, and I found myself smirking. I jumped to my feet and made my way out of my secret garden, I looked back at the nettle patch, making a mental reminder to myself of their location for future reference.

I'd reached my verdict on Sydney, now all I had to do was fill her in on it.

I walked into my room, Brianna and Taylor were sitting on the bed playing snap and Sydney was laid out on her bed, her headphones were in, and she was scrolling through her phone. I strode over to her bed, leaned over and yanked out one of her headphones.

"What do you think you're doing, these are designer?" she glared at me.

"Whatever," I rolled my eyes. "I want to talk, follow me." I waved her over.

I walked off confidently across the room without looking back at her. As I walked out into the corridor, I didn't have to turn around to know that she was following me. I smirked to myself as I carried on walking. I walked to the very end of the corridor where the rooms were being decorated so it was usually quieter here and I carried on until I reached the staircase. I sat down on the top step, soon someone sat down next to me. I turned and smiled at Sydney.

“What is it?” she gave me a questioning look.

"I've been thinking, and I've decided that I want to be your friend."

“Really?” Sydney raised an eyebrow.

“Yes, really,” I shrugged. “I mean, I could be your enemy but what’s the point? I don’t want an enemy, especially not one as good at pranks as you are. Besides, I’d rather have you on my team. So, what do you say?” I looked at her.

“This isn't a joke?” she gave me a skeptical look. “I mean, I don't want to say yes then have kids jump out at me and cover me in slime or something.”

“No joke and no slime, I promise.” I chuckled.

“Well then yes, I’d like to be your friend.” Sydney smiled and held out her hand.

I quickly shook it and said, “Good, now go and get me a glass of water.”

I could see the annoyance on her face, she was about to reply when I burst into laughter.

“Got ya!” I burst into laughter.

“No, I so knew you were joking.” Sydney laughed as she shook her head.

“I bet you’ve never had a friend like me before?” I grinned.

“I suppose not. I bet you’ve never had a friend like me?”

“I guess not.”

We exchanged awkward looks and then glanced away from

each other. I was never shy or uncomfortable or any of those things, but I didn't know how to be around Sydney. She wasn't like the other girls, she was different.

“I hated this place at first,” I carried on looking away from Sydney. “I was bullied; badly. I rang my mom up and told her I wanted to come home. She told me to toughen up, and that the world was hard at times and if I were going to be a wimp, I'd be bullied my whole life. So, over the next couple of years, she coached me on how to stand up for myself and become the alpha girl in my class. My mom really is amazing, she's super smart and tough, and no one ever messes with her, she taught me a lot.”

“Really? I couldn't imagine you ever being bullied.” Sydney replied.

“Yeah, I know, it's hard to believe, isn't it?” I looked over at her and grinned. “But it's true. Boarding school is all I know, I've been going to them since I was a little kid; I was only five. I didn't like being away from my parents, but it forced me to grow up fast.”

“That's so young!” Sydney sounded shocked. “Why did they send you away when you were that age?”

“They're both super successful and busy. Mom and Dad were always at work, and I barely saw them. They employed this nanny called Samantha, but she was a proper suck-up when they were around, but as soon as they left, she showed no interest in me. She used to put some boring film on for me to watch and go off and ring up her friends and her boyfriend. I was so lonely, it was horrible. At the time, I thought that my parents were normal, but I see how other parents are with their kids, and they act completely different from how mine do. Take Brianna's mom; for instance, she rings her every night.”

"Yeah and you tease her about it," Sydney quipped.

"I guess I'm jealous. Don't tell Brianna that I said that though." I glared at Sydney.

"I won't," Sydney sighed. "I guess I'm a little jealous too."

"Maybe we're both so strong-minded because of our parents? Maybe it's a good thing that they suck at times," I smirked.

"Maybe. It's so much better than being as lame as Taylor, does that girl even have her own mind?" Sydney asked.

"I'm waiting for the day she'll suddenly snap and go crazy at me," I chuckled.

"It'll never happen."

"I don't blame her, I am an intimidating force," I replied.

Sydney smirked as she shook her head.

"I'm glad I'm not like Taylor or Brianna or any of the others. They are so boring and predictable."

"Yeah, they are, but they're good to have onside. Those two girls will do whatever you want and hang on your every word. I used to have friends like that back in my last school." Sydney thought about her old school friends.

"What was it like? I mean, not being at boarding school. I couldn't imagine what it'd be like to go home every day after lessons finished."

"Yeah, it was okay. I guess..." Sydney tilted her head to the side. "I used to think it was so lame but compared to this place there was so much variety and freedom."

"So lame that you set fire to your house." I regretted it as soon as I said it. “Sorry.” I looked down at my knees.

“That really was an accident.” Sydney sighed. “My mom is a health freak, so my friends and I decided to cook some spring rolls while she wasn’t around, but it went wrong.” She rubbed the burn mark on her arm.

“You should be allowed to eat junk food sometimes, you’re a kid.”

“Yeah, well that’s the good thing about being here. I can eat cake, even if it is dry and has crunchy bits in it.” Sydney smiled.

“Yeah, that cake isn’t the best,” I chuckled. “There’s always food in my house, so I just eat whatever I want. My parents are never there though, as they are always at work. I get so bored, and there are only so many candy bars I can eat to pass the time. The only kid who lives near me, who is my age, is this annoying girl with pink braces and bad pores, sometimes I get so bored I end up hanging out with her. And if you tell anyone that, I will put worms in your pillowcase.” I grinned.

“I won’t.” She looked at me. “What’s said on the staircase stays on the staircase, I pinkie promise.” Sydney held her pinkie out to me.

“Pinkie promise.” I leaned over and wrapped my pinkie around hers.

“Parents, they are a pain,” Sydney said sighing.

“Yeah, they are,” I sighed back. “I just accepted my upbringing as normal, but now I’m older, I think that my parents never really wanted me.”

“Mine neither,” Sydney muttered. “Well, I think my dad cares about me, but he’s too weak to ever stand up to my mom."

"My mom cares about the family reputation more, that and money. She thinks that everything can be solved with money. In my bid to be the top dog, I got into loads of trouble, and I nearly got expelled. Mom wrote out a large cheque, and that was the problem solved."

"My mom thinks money solves everything too. She has all the money she could dream of, but nothing ever seems good enough for her; I'm not good enough for her," she gave a thoughtful sigh.

"Yeah well, their money and endless cheques mean we are pretty much untouchable," I gave a devious grin. "Take me for instance, I'm the original wild child, and everyone knows not to mess with me."

"Wild child, I like it." Sydney smiled.

"Yeah me too." I smiled back.

I didn't know why I'd told the new girl all this. It was only earlier today that I was deliberating if I should be her friend or her enemy, yet I'd basically just told her my life story. Jeez, what was going on with me?

Although I had to admit that just for once it was nice not having to keep up my tough girl persona. It took a lot of energy to be the strong, sassy version of me, sometimes I just wanted to admit that I was vulnerable too. Although I was never a wimpy, let-people-walk-all-over-me type of vulnerable, not like how Taylor and most of the other girls were. I mean, I'm still me, I'm still the infamous wild child, and that was never going to change.

At first, I wasn't sure if Harper's offer of peace was a set-up or not…as that girl took sneaky and manipulative to whole new levels. But even she couldn't be that cruel, could she? She'd opened up to me, even though I could tell that talking about personal stuff was hard for her. We actually had a lot of similarities, we were both strong-minded, super smart for our age, pretty (although I was prettier) and we were both leaders. We also had lame, money-obsessed parents. Mine were bad, but Harper's seemed even worse. They sent her away to boarding school at five, even my parents didn't do that. Back at that age, I got tucked into bed every night by someone, even if it was my nanny. Being in a place like this at such a young age would be terrifying. No wonder Harper was like she was, she'd adapted to her surroundings, and now she'd learned to thrive in them.

She may have put me through some pretty mean tests, but it was all about showing that she was in charge. I didn't want to be enemies with her, I wanted to be her friend. I mean, I was strong and everything, but I really didn't like the idea of having Harper as an enemy. I didn't want to be continually looking over my shoulder and worrying about what horrible trick she had lined up for me next. She ruled the school, so messing with her was a bad idea. I was still finding my feet, and as amazing as I was, she had a massive head start on me. Yeah, being friends with her made way more sense, although there was no way I would ever be her lapdog, like Brianna and Taylor were.

I looked at Harper, she was still sitting on the step, her legs were crossed, and she had on her usual tough-girl look, but I saw a different look in her eyes; a dash of vulnerability. Before I could even stop myself, I scooted along until I was close to her and then I placed my arm around her shoulders and brought her in for a hug.

No, I don't know what possessed me to do such a thing either. Maybe I'd drunk too much orange juice that morning or something, who knows. Harper flinched and gave me a funny look. I smiled at her and continued with the hug and Harper's posture softened. She suddenly started to sob quietly. I didn't know what to do at first, but then I gently patted her on the back.

"Harper, it's all going to be alright. You are I are going to make the best team EVER!"

She dabbed at the corner of her eyes with her finger and then looked at me through glassy eyes. "Yeah, I think we are." She managed a smile.

Chapter Two - Acceptance

I am not a weak person, I know that, and I know that you do too. The fact I'd opened up to Sydney made me feel uneasy, but as I saw it, I had two choices, (again!) I could either go back to being mean to her to show how strong I was. Or, I could just see how this whole friendship thing with her went. I could have easily been mean to her, I had so many pranks in my head that I could have ordered the other girls to carry out, but to-be-honest I wasn't feeling it. My gut was telling me to give Sydney a chance, so I guess that was what I was going to do.

After my talk with Sydney, I went off and did my own thing for the rest of the day. I spent most of it in the library making sure that I was ahead on my homework and when I finished that, I spent a fair while doodling pictures on the back page of my notebook. I went back to my room before dinner and Sydney was there, so we both walked with linked arms to the cafeteria. Everyone was staring at us as we walked in, Zoe even dropped her fork. Sydney and I exchanged smirks before we walked over to the food line. We placed our trays down next to each other and glanced at the confused looking other girls.

"I thought you hated each other?" Amy stared at us open-mouthed.

"Nah," I shrugged. "I've never hated Sydney."

"But you said," Zoe muttered.

"I never said I hated her." I glared at Zoe. "I had to put her through the initiation test as rules-are-rules," I smirked.

"I guess." Zoe looked down at her plate of mash.

"You certainly acted like you hated her," Amy added.

Jeez, that girl seriously had no filters.

"Syd and I have always been friends." I grinned.

Taylor started choking on her food and Brianna patted her on the back. Suddenly a piece of half-chewed chicken flew out of her mouth, hit me in the face and then fell onto my tray.

There was a brief silence as both Taylor and Brianna looked from me to the piece of mangled up food in horror. I kept a stern face before I grinned and then burst into laughter. Soon Sydney, Brianna, Taylor, and the other girls all started to laugh too. Even Miss Crombie laughed as she walked past our table.

So, I had to admit that I felt good. I was glad that Sydney and I had reached an agreement. I was sure that when we put both our minds together, we would certainly liven up this boring old school.

Monday morning arrived and bought with it the first class of the day, history; yawn! Harper had a meeting with some of the sixth form kids, so I was walking to class ahead of Brianna and Taylor. Suddenly they sidled up either side of me, and Brianna coughed to clear her voice.

“Hey Syd, look, um, Taylor, and I wanted to talk to you about something.” Brianna stared down at her feet.

I was convinced that it was going to be something terrible like they didn't like me being friends with Harper, and they were going to tell me that I wasn't allowed to hang out with her.

“What is it?” I snapped.

"Um, well," Brianna spluttered. "Look, we're both super sorry, okay, I mean, for being mean to you. We didn't want to be, but Harper told us to do it and, well, she can be really scary at times."

I raised an eyebrow, I mean, she seemed to be genuine and all, but I didn't trust these girls.

"Yeah, we're both sorry." Taylor gave me a sheepish look. "Harper was really mean to us when we first started here, and it's easier to just do as she asks."

"Yeah, when I first started, she stole all my underwear, and I had to go everywhere without any on for two whole days. Harper told the other girls, and they all laughed at me and made mean comments, it was really embarrassing," Brianna said blushing.

"At least you had the rest of your school uniform to hide your underwear problem. Harper took all of my shoes, so I had to go to class with bare feet. When the teacher asked where my shoes were, Harper butted in and told her that my parents were hippies and that I'd never worn them before and that the teacher didn't need to worry as she'd train me how to be a lady." Taylor shuddered at the memory.

"It's okay girls." I gave a weak smile. "I know exactly how *mean* some girls can be. There was this horrible girl at my last school called Remmy. All I wanted to be was her friend, but she went out of her way to be nasty to me. This boy, called Charlie, really liked me and wanted me to be his girlfriend, but Remmy wanted him for herself. She was so horrible, and it was super traumatic but I'm away from her now, and I'd really like for us all to be friends."

"That's awful!" Brianna gave me a sympathetic look. "Girls can be so mean. But it'll be better now and I'm really sorry about the way I treated you when you arrived."

She pulled me in for a hug.

"And me." Taylor hugged us both.

They eventually pulled away, and I saw the goofy smiles on their faces.

"We're going to be the best of friends." Brianna giggled excitedly.

"It's so good having amazing friends." I gave them both my best sincere look.

Okay, so being publicly hugged by two of Harper's slaves wasn't the coolest thing ever but I'd take it over being enemies with them. Besides, I guess they both had their uses, I mean Brianna was good with hair and Taylor was an alright artist. Having a circle full of people with different skills was always a good idea as there might be a time when they'd come in handy. It'd also be handy having them about to follow my orders. I mean I'd go about it in a much nicer way than Harper does, at least that's what I'd do at first.

***

I sat by Harper in every class that morning, and she was super sweet to me. She even loaned me a pencil when the nib on mine broke (I had spares in my pencil case, but she didn't know that.) It felt good not worrying what horrible thing they were going to do next, instead, it was nice to have them being cool.

We were all chatting happily together at lunch when the famous ditch-me-at-the-mall threesome strolled over to me. I feigned interest in my on-the-verge-of-stale-sandwich as I pretended not to notice them.

"Hey, Sydney," called out Tiff.

I took another bite of my sandwich before I looked at them and chewed really slowly.

"We just wanted to say no hard feelings about the mall prank." Tiff smiled at me.

I continued to chew on my food.

"So yeah, are we cool?"

I paused for a few seconds for added effect.

"Yeah, we're cool." I gave a broad smile.

"Oh great, I mean, what doesn't break you makes you stronger and all that jazz."

"Yeah, doesn't it just," I muttered under my breath. I made sure to maintain my smile.

Tiff gave me another smile and a feeble wave before she spun around and walked off. Grace and Hannah both smiled at me before they followed her. Harper nudged me in the arm, so I looked at her, and she looked from Tiff and her friends to me and then rolled her eyes. I chuckled and then shook my head, and the other girls at our table laughed too.

I mean, I liked a bit of drama to keep things interesting, but maybe peace returning to my life was a good thing, at least for now....

Chapter Three - Exciting Times

The worst thing about this stupid school was the lack of boys. Even though most boys were kind of gross, they didn't brush their teeth regularly, they liked getting dirty, and they found lame jokes funny. Still, being surrounded by girls was tiresome and boring at times. I did miss sitting in class and having a cute boy or two to look at. Also, I hadn't seen Elliot, Mr. Meuler's cute son since one of Harper's initiation tests meant I had to get a photo taken with him. The other girls talked about boys a lot, especially Brianna. It was as though they were this alien species to them, which I found amusing. I guess none of them were used to them, and that wasn't surprising seeing as they were stuck in this place.

I was sitting between Harper and Taylor in one of Miss Braun's usual drone-on assemblies when suddenly everyone else began to cheer. Like, seriously, why? All she did was mention some stupid dance with some school called Aquinas. Was everyone that zombied out in this decrepit old school that even some stupid old dance seemed exciting to them?

"What's going on?" I whispered to Harper.

"Aquinas is a boys' school, it's easy to send these girls into an over-excitement mode," she rolled her eyes.

Brianna was still clapping her hands together and squealing, like seriously, had she never seen a boy before or something?

"I guess some of them are cute looking and it's nice to have something new to look at," Harper commented.

"I'm so excited," Brianna squealed. "This is the BEST day ever!"

I rolled my eyes, I guess I could see the appeal to being around boys, but Brianna was, well, she was being Brianna. She jumped up to her feet and was clapping her hands together like an enthusiastic seal. Everyone else had calmed down and fallen silent except for her. Everyone and I mean EVERYONE in the assembly hall was looking at her. I turned my head to the side as their judgmental eyes made me cringe. I felt like standing up and announcing that I didn't know her, had never seen her before and would never see her again.

"Ahem," Miss Braun thundered.

Still, Brianna was too excited to catch the hint. Eventually, Taylor tugged on Brianna's arm and pulled her back down into her seat.

"What?" Brianna looked at her. "Aren't you excited about seeing boys?"

"Yes, but everyone's staring at you," she said through gritted teeth.

Brianna gazed around her and saw that everyone was looking and laughing at her.

"Oh!" She giggled. "It is exciting about the boys though; I feel like I haven't seen one in years."

I rolled my eyes again and laughed to myself. Brianna was ditsy, a little on the stupid side at times and she giggled at almost everything. Still, she was kind of funny, and as I sat there, I couldn't help but find myself smiling at her actions.

Assembly ended and study time started. Yeah, as if that was going to happen! Boys, boys, boys, boys, boys. I skimmed through my math homework as I listened to the other girls go through a list of the best boys as Aquinas.

"Connor Ellis is cute, and his parents own their own island," Harper said.

"He never dances though, he just sits there, drinking squash and swiping his hand through his floppy hair," Taylor commented.

Harper glared at her and Taylor blushed and then sank further down on her desk chair.

"Benji Henley is so cute," Brianna said.

"No, he's not, he's got acne." Harper snorted.

"So, he's still cute."

"Zack Forrester and Davey Baxter are both kind of cute in certain lights," Harper flicked her hair behind her back. "I mean I've seen cuter boys on vacation, but for Aquinas, they aren't bad."

"I think Elliot Meuler is really cute," Brianna commented.

My ears pricked at the mention of his name.

"You mean the janitors son?" I tried to sound as casual as I could.

"Yeah, that's him. Of course, you've already met him. The photo challenge and all," she smiled at me.

"Yeah," I muttered.

"He has a massssiiiivvveeee crush on Harper."

Great! Why did the cute boys always end up liking someone else?

"Mr. Meuler works two jobs so that he can send him to Aquinas. He doesn't board though, he's a day student," Harper said.

"He's super good looking, I wish he was my boyfriend." Brianna giggled.

"You're dreaming again, Brianna. Elliot wouldn't be interested in you." Harper smirked.

"I only said I wished." Brianna's face dropped.

I watched as she slumped down onto her bed and feigned interest in her homework. Okay, so Harper was probably right, a boy as cute as Elliot wouldn't be interested in someone like Brianna but Harper didn't have to tell her that. It was a pretty cruel putdown.

"Bree, don't forget Logan Jeffries and Tim Hodgkins." Taylor said, trying to smooth over the situation.

"Oh yes," Brianna seemed to perk up. "I wouldn't mind being a girlfriend to either of them."

"As if." Harper snorted while rolling her eyes in a very obvious insult.

Brianna looked even more deflated, and I found myself actually feeling bad for her.

"I suppose I could help you." The words tumbled out of my mouth. "I mean, I guess I could be your coach."

"Really?" Brianna's eyes widened in excitement.

"Yeah, I don't see why not." I shrugged.

Brianna darted off her bed, ran over to me and flung her arms around me. "Thank you, thank you, thank you," she squealed.

She was squeezing me so hard that I felt like I'd been mummified.

"Bree," I croaked, almost out of breath.

"Oh, sorry." She giggled as she let go of me. "Would you seriously do that for me?"

"I suppose I can give it a go. I mean, after all, I am pretty good at attracting boys." I gave a wide smile.

"I'm going to get a boyfriend, I'm going to get a boyfriend, and he's going to be the cutest, and I'm going to get a boyfriend," Brianna sang out, as she bounced around the bedroom.

"Lesson one," I commented, and Brianna instantly fell quiet. "You have to be cool about boys. The harder you try, the more you will scare them away."

"Yeah, um, okay." Brianna gave me a hopeful look before she continued singing and dancing around the room again. "I'm going to get a boyfriend, I'm going to get a boyfriend, and he's going to be the hottest, and I'm going to get a boyfriend."

I shook my head, why had I agreed to help her? This was going to be difficult. No, scrap that, this was going to be on the verge of impossible.

"Good luck with that." Harper smirked over at me. "You're definitely going to need it."

Harper

Finally, another dance!!! The last one was three months ago, although it felt like three years. I was relieved that it hadn't actually been three years, as the previous three months with Brianna starved from boys was bad enough. Jeez, that girl was unbearable at times. As if a boy would even notice her over girls like Sydney and me. I mean, I suppose she wasn't ugly or anything, but she was somewhat plain looking, and she was seriously annoying at times.

Anyway, I was looking forward to the dance. I got so fed up seeing the spotty faces of the other girls and the wrinkled faces of the teachers…boring! A few cute boys to look at would definitely be favorable, and of course, all of the boys would be looking at me! I liked the attention, I mean, who wouldn't? At the last dance, Elliot asked me to dance, and I'd agreed because, well, why not? He was cute I guess, and it was worth doing just to annoy Brianna, as no boy ever wanted to dance with her. She was far too giggly and excitable; they were probably afraid that she would stand on their feet.

Okay, so maybe, secretly I did like Elliot. I couldn't deny that seeing him pose in that picture with Sydney on the initiation test did annoy me. I'd decided then that the best thing to do was to pretend that I didn't know him. I've danced with lots of boys from Aquinas, but he was the only one who thanked me afterward. Also, he had the cutest smile. I was going to make him my boyfriend, I was sure of it. Then Brianna and the other girls could stop talking about him like that. He was going to be mine. They could go and fight over the other boys all they wanted, but Elliot was taken, and they needed to leave him alone!

Chapter Four - The Lessons Begin

The following morning Brianna sat cross-legged on my bed and looked at me with her big rabbit eyes. She was humming happily to herself. Part of me wanted to help her, but the other part wanted to push her off my bed. Why did I agree to help her? When it came to boys, some girls had the gift of luring them in, it came naturally to them, as if it was a part of their DNA. Brianna did not have this gift. Instead, I was pretty sure that she probably had boy repellent genes.

"Okay, so I'm going to teach you a new lesson every morning before breakfast for the next six days. If you follow my advice…by the end of my lessons, you should at least be semi-cool." I looked at her.

"I'd like to see that." Harper peered up from her book and smirked at me.

"Thank you, thank you, thank you," Brianna squealed out as she clapped her hands together. "I'm so excited, I can't wait to be cool and for boys to like me."

Oh, help me! Was this girl for real? She reminded me of a naive puppy who constantly chased its tail. The difference was that puppies grew up and calmed down, I imagined that Brianna would still be bouncing around like Tigger when she was thirty.

I gently grabbed her arms so that she remained still for once.

"Okay, so firstly you need to calm down. Boys don't like the whole clapping like a seal thing," I told her.

"Oh!" she giggled. "I can do that."

"Great," I let go of her arms. "So, lesson one. Confidence is the key! Boys want a girl who knows her own mind and who isn't afraid to be herself." Brianna was giving me a doe-eyed look. "Well, a cool version of herself."

"I can do that," she said giggling.

"Yeah," I sighed. "Sure, you can."

I watched as she peered around the room, clapped her hands together, realized she did it, then stopped and chewed on her lip, then clapped her hands together again. I liked a challenge, but this was going to be far from easy, which I knew Harper was well aware of, which was why she kept on peering over her book and smiling at me.

"Okay, the easiest way of doing this is to pretend that I'm a boy you don't know."

"That's easy as I don't know any boys." She giggled.

"Great." I gritted my teeth. "So, which boy do you have a crush on?"

"Um, I like Elliot, as he's the cutest and the nicest." She giggled again.

I raised an eyebrow at the mention of Elliot's name. I looked over at Harper, she was peering over her book opened-mouthed. Did her reaction mean that she liked Elliot too? Great, why did everyone have to like the same boy as me? They were just going to have to deal with it, as they weren't going to win this battle. I turned my attention back to Brianna who was waiting for me to tell her what to do next. I was beginning to think that I was crazy for ever offering to help her. Maybe the air in this decrepit old school was turning me loopy?

"Okay, so pretend I'm Elliot."

Brianna let out a squeal, flicked out her hair and then giggled again. She hopped off my bed, walked over to the door, spun around and then with her hand on her hip she did a weird trying-too-hard waddle over to me.

"Hi there gorgeous, I'm Brianna, and I really like you." She swished her head to the side.

Harper burst out laughing, she ended up dropping her book and clutching her stomach, but still, she continued to laugh. Taylor was rolling around on the floor, her laughter was also uncontrollable. I shook my head and tried to hold back my laughter, but it wasn't easy.

"What's so funny?" She gave me a confused look.

“Do you want to impress him or scare him off forever?” I asked.

“She’ll be asking to marry him next!” Harper laughed out.

“Too full on?” Brianna asked.

“A little,” I replied.

“A LOT,” Harper shouted.

Brianna looked deflated. Her shoulders sagged, and for once she wasn't giggly. She perched on the edge of my bed and let out a long sigh.

“I know nothing about boys. I’m useless with them, so useless that I’m never going to get a boyfriend. I’m going to die a lonely old spinster who has forty-seven cats, wears clothing that clashes in color and terribly sensible shoes.”

We all giggled at this, even Brianna, although hers was more of a nervous thing.

“It's a genuine fear,” she gave a solemn giggle. “I often dream about my future, and it features a huge house overrun with cats and threadbare furniture.” She shuddered at the thought.

I leaned over and placed my hand on her shoulder.

“You will not be a cat woman,” I reassured her. “Now focus. You have a lot to learn and only a week to do it in.”

“Thank you,” she nodded her head.

Brianna reminded me of one of those annoying nodding dogs that some equally annoying people put in the back window of their cars.

“First off, you need to learn to calm down. Luckily for you, I had a yoga-obsessed mom, so I know all about breathing techniques," I said.

Harper and Taylor both started laughing, so I looked over at them, my eyebrows raised.

"You can both do it too," I remarked.

"No chance am I partaking in your hippy nonsense," Harper snorted.

"We are meant to be supporting Brianna."

"I'll do it." Taylor walked over to us and sat down on the floor next to my bed.

"Okay then, make sure you sit with your back straight," I replied.

"Wait," Harper called out. "I suppose I could try it too."

"Great," I announced.

She swayed her way over to my bed and sat down next to Brianna. She straightened her posture and relaxed her arms by her side.

"Now, close your eyes," I instructed, and they all did as I asked. "Remember to keep sitting straight, now relax your body. Inhale through your nose like this." I breathed in through my nose. "Then exhale out through your mouth for longer." I breathed out.

I listened to the girls as they breathed in and out.

"Great, now this time breathe in deeper, so that your stomach expands with air. Then breathe out." I demonstrated.

"Do I have to do this heavy breathing when I talk to Elliot?"

Brianna asked.

"No," I chuckled. "You should do this beforehand to help calm your nerves."

"Oh, okay." She giggled.

Harper placed the back of her hand against her forehead and pretended to faint as she fell back onto my bed. Taylor burst out laughing, Brianna looked at her confused, and I just rolled my eyes. It was nice to see that Harper thought this was a joke, then again, she was probably right. Brianna was a lost cause, there was probably more chance of my mom showing up and taking me home than Brianna ever getting a boyfriend. Luckily for her, I wasn't a quitter.

"If the breathing exercises don't work then go and dance by yourself to a few songs to wear off your nervous energy," I leaned in closer to Brianna so that only she could hear me. "Boys love confident girls," I whispered.

"Boys love confident girls," she repeated under her breath.

"When you feel settled walk confidently over to him with your shoulders straight and a smile on your face."

Brianna arched back her shoulders and grinned like a Cheshire cat.

"A slight smile, like this." I gave her my best half smile.

She tried to copy me, but she was trying so hard that her right eye ended up twitching. Harper and Taylor started laughing, and I sighed to myself.

"Yeah, you might want to work on that. Anyway, walk over to him, look him straight in the eye." I looked directly at her. "And say, *hi, my name's Brianna.*"

"Okay," she nodded. "I can do that."

She walked over to the door and breathed in through her nose and out through her mouth before she began.

"This is going to be hilarious," Harper whispered under her breath.

Brianna strode over to me with a weird robot-like stride, squinted at me as she tried to keep a demure smile and then tripped over her own feet and nearly knocked me over.

Harper and Taylor were in hysterics, but Brianna stood up and carried on.

"Um, Hi, my name's Brianna," she said in a high-pitched tone.

"What was that?" Harper placed her hands over her ears. "You sound like someone's pulling your hair." She laughed.

I could see Brianna's eyes tearing up.

"I'm never going to get it." She sniffed.

I gave Harper and Taylor dirty looks, they seriously weren't helping the situation with their constant jibes and laughter.

"Come on." I put my arm around Brianna and led her back over to the door. "Copy me."

I held my shoulders back, gave my best half smile and confidently walked over to Harper. Brianna followed me, but she was still doing that weird robot walk.

"Stand up straighter and walk more normally," I instructed.

She did as I said and although she was still a complete disaster, she looked less robot-like.

"Hi, my name's Brianna." I said and stopped in front of Harper.

"Sorry but I'm not into losers," she teased.

I smiled at her before I swished my hair behind my back and then walked off.

"Your turn," I said to Brianna.

She gave a nod before she stopped in front of Taylor (I didn't blame her for not walking up to Harper.)

"Hi," she gave a twitchy-eyed smile.

"Okay, just smile normally," I said.

She gave her Cheshire cat look again.

"A bit less."

She softened her smile and managed to hold it without twitching her eye.

"Great." I smiled. "Now, carry on."

"Hi, I'm Brianna." She looked straight at an uneasy looking Taylor.

"Um, hi," Taylor grunted.

"What was that?" Harper mimicked her before she burst out laughing.

"I was pretending to be Elliot!" Taylor blushed.

"Since when has Elliot sounded like he has a permanent cold?" Harper continued to laugh.

"That was much better Brianna." I ignored Harper. "Now this time do it without following me."

She gave a nervous nod before she walked back over to the door. I forced a smile as I watched her walk like a robot, again-and-again-and-again. By her eighth try, I was about ready to scream, and even Harper had gone from finding it amusing to looking bored out of her brains.

"Okay Bree, one last time." I tried to sound positive.

"Okay." she skipped her way back over to the door.

Harper pressed two fingers against her temple, and mouthed *boom!* And then she sprawled out on the bed. Taylor giggled to herself, and I rolled my eyes. She did have a point though; this was growing tedious.

"Okay, so remember that confidence is key." I smiled over at her. "You've got this, Brianna."

"Right, I've got this," she said to herself.

She walked towards me with a walk that no longer resembled a robot. Instead, it was verging on graceful. The smile on her face was intriguing without being too much, and her eye wasn't twitching. She stopped in front of me and looked me straight in the eye.

"Hi there, I'm Brianna," she said assertively.

There was a pause before I gave her a smile back.

"That was brilliant!"

Harper and Taylor were both cheering, and Brianna had a massive grin on her face.

"Finally, now let's go to breakfast." Harper stood up.

Brianna's smile fell.

"We'll catch up," I told them.

"Whatever." Harper rolled her eyes before she linked her arm through Taylor's and led her towards the door.

I waited until they'd left before I spoke. "So, what's up?" I asked.

"It's just, what do I say to him if he replies?" Brianna asked.

Seriously, she was upset over this? Was this girl really that clueless? I sighed to myself, knowing that I already knew the answer to that.

"Well, he may ask you a question, or he may say nothing. If he asks you a question then you should just answer in a natural voice, remember that you want to pretend that you're cool."

The door swung open, and Harper strolled back into the room, and I saw Taylor lingering in the doorway.

"I forgot my chap-stick." She grinned as she opened her bedside cabinet and rummaged through it.

"But what if he doesn't say anything?" Brianna asked.

"Well, then you ask him a question to get the conversation going."

"But what do I ask him? I'm blank, even in here I don't know what to say! So, what's going to happen when I stand in front of the cutest boy ever? I'm going to be a complete mess."

"Ask him if he thinks I'm hot," Harper said before she pouted and applied chap-stick.

I gave her a death stare, seriously, why did she have to be so unhelpful? Ask him if he's enjoying the dance or even what his favorite song is. You can ask him whatever pops into your head."

"Oooh, I could ask him what his favorite animal is," Brianna said enthusiastically.

Harper laughed.

"Um, maybe you should write down a list of possible questions and show me first."

"Thanks, Sydney."

"That's okay. Try to think up stuff that you have in common, such as what it's like going to a same-sex school?"

"I can't say the *sex* word to him!" Brianna looked horrified.

Harper burst out laughing again, and I struggled not to do the same.

"Okay, you could ask him what his school is like. You know, does he like his school? What's his favorite subject? What are the teachers like? Then if he replies you could mention some of the strange teachers we have here."

"We certainly have those," Harper commented.

"Remember that you have to talk too, the conversation needs to flow between you both. You can't just bombard him with questions."

"Okay, I think I need to practice that before the dance," she gave a meek reply.

"Good idea!" Harper yelled, as she walked across the room.

"It would make a good reality TV series." Taylor laughed from the doorway. "How to Catch That Boy!"

"Can we please get to breakfast before I lose the will to live,"

Harper remarked.

"You didn't have to come back," I replied.

"Yeah, well, I can't abide having dry lips." Harper smirked and air kissed me.

As we walked towards the door, Brianna sidled up next to me.

"Thanks so much, Sydney." She smiled.

"That's okay," I replied.

She smiled again before she hurried over to Taylor. Harper lingered back and then walked alongside me.

"I think what you're doing for Brianna is really nice. Hopeless but nice. You do realize that she will be a disaster on the night, right?" She grinned at me.

"Maybe, maybe not." I smiled. "I guess time will tell."

"It certainly will." She smirked.

I maintained my smile. Part of me wanted Brianna to ace this…just to wipe the smug look off Harper's face, but at the same time Brianna couldn't end up with Elliot. I was the one that was going to end up with him. In all honesty, I wasn't worried about Brianna stealing my guy, at the most he would talk to her just to be nice. Harper, on the other hand, was smart, pretty and determined. If she had her sights set on Elliot, then there could be trouble. What she needed to realize was that it just so happened that I was smarter, prettier and I was used to getting what I wanted.

Chapter Five - Cupcakes

The cooking class was pointless, seriously pointless. As if I needed to know how to make some stupid food over learning real subjects like Math and English? The other girls liked cooking class because it was easy, but I wanted a challenge, I wanted to learn, I wanted to feel like each lesson meant something.

So, there I was sitting at a workbench next to a giggling Brianna. Naturally, this was her favorite class, but then she lacked the brain cells needed for the more challenging subjects. I stared out of the window and watched as one of the gardeners rode along on his lawnmower. Right now, I would rather be out there! I'd much rather the aroma of freshly cut grass over being in this stuffy classroom and being forced to cook. Who cooks these days? Nobody!

"Today is a very exciting day." Ms. Ekelby clapped her hands together.

Great, another seal, just what I needed…not!!!

"You're going to be making cupcakes for the school dance." She clapped again.

Brianna squealed as she transformed into full-on seal mode. I only just managed to duck in time to avoid getting an elbow in the face. "Watch it," I growled at her.

"Sorry!" She giggled some more.

The other girls cheered enthusiastically but that was only because the dance had been mentioned. I mean seriously, cupcakes. This wasn't the olden days, cupcakes definitely needed to be left in the last decade, no, century!

The more I thought about it, the more annoyed I grew. This was a $70 000 a year school, yet there we were making cupcakes. Seriously, couldn't they just buy them from the local bakery or something? This lesson felt like such a waste of time and effort.

"Excuse me Ms. Ekelby," I called out. "Making cupcakes is beneath me. When in my normal life would I ever make cupcakes?" I asked sarcastically.

Everyone stared at me, shocked looks on their faces. I just shrugged at them, a smirk on my face. Ms. Elkelby looked flustered, I could tell that she was deliberating how best to answer. I found it amusing how dithery she was. Where did they find this woman? Was there a shortage of teachers or something?

“Well Harper, I’d assume that you may have guests over occasionally. Or perhaps one day you may have children and want to prepare some cupcakes for their lunch or afternoon tea.” She stared at me, her cheeks flushed.

I stood up, flicked back my hair and then placed my hand on my hip. “Miss, that’s a whole lot of assumptions going on there.”

“And what is wrong with making cupcakes, Harper?” she failed to mask the nerves from her voice.

“My parents pay a lot of money for me to be educated at this school, I don’t think making cupcakes would be on their highly prized skills list,” I said snidely.

Ms. Elkelby stared back at me dumbfounded. She had no idea how to reply, probably because she knew that I was right.

“Cut it out Harper.” Emma came to the teacher's defense. “Nobody cares if you'll ever make cupcakes again or not.”

Trust Emma to choose now to voice her stupid opinion. I couldn't stand the girl; she was so goody-two-shoes and boring. The annoying thing was that she was strong-willed with it which meant that we clashed. Sometimes I liked raising a reaction out of her, other times I just wanted her to shut up. Right now, I wanted her to do the latter.

"Nobody asked for your pathetic opinion, Emma, so back off!" I yelled at her.

"Says the girl who craves attention," she retaliated.

"You can open a cupcake shop if you want to, but I have bigger ambitions for my life."

"Such as bullying people until you get your own way," Emma replied sarcastically.

The other girls were following our argument, their heads turning from me and then to Emma as the insults were hurled.

"Enough," Ms. Elkelby slammed her hand down onto the workbench. "You will learn how to make cupcakes, and you will help us to bake them or you won't be going to the dance!"

I stared at the teacher, noticing how the vein on her neck was pulsing so much it looked like it was going to burst. She was usually so sweet and naïve, which made her an easy target. I had to admit that I was kind of impressed.

I definitely didn't think Ms. Elkelby had any fire in her, turns out she was harboring a volcano. She had me cornered, as I badly wanted to go to the dance and see Elliot again. I could not leave him to be smothered by the likes of Brianna. Making lame cupcakes was a small price to pay if it meant seeing him again.

I shrugged my shoulders. "Okay, I'll learn how to make stupid cupcakes." Under my breath, I whispered, "But it's a total waste of time."

Trust Harper to make a scene. Yeah, so okay, making cupcakes wasn't the highlight of my day either, but it was just one stupid lesson. She did it because she liked irritating the teachers. I suppose it made her feel powerful.

Until now, Emma hadn't featured much on my radar. I mean, she was prettyish, smartish and she seemed a typical follow-the-rules kind of student. She had really held her own against Harper though, and that was no easy feat. What's more, I now knew Harper's weakness. She really wanted to go to the dance, enough to give in and spend the lesson making cupcakes. I stored this fact in my mind, just in case I needed some ammunition, later on.

“Okay then, let’s get started,” Ms. Elkelby’s tone had returned back to her jittery, nervous normality. “Please, can you all get into pairs.”

Out of the corner of my eye, I saw a figure dart across the room towards me.

“Sydney, you’re my partner,” Harper announced, as she gripped my arm.

Great! I was partnered up with the cupcake hating queen herself. I resisted the urge to roll my eyes and instead I smiled sweetly at her.

The worst bit about today was we didn’t get to eat the cupcakes. Making them for other people didn’t have the same appeal, even if some of those people were cute boys such as Elliot. I found myself wondering if he preferred chocolate frosting or strawberry swirl?

“Sydney. Earth to Sydney.” Harper waved a laminated recipe card in front of me. “Ms. Elkelby just handed me this.” Harper deliberately moved it away from me and studied it.

“I’m not going to demonstrate today as they’re easy to make. *And I’m now short on time,*” Ms., Elkelby said under her breath. “Please, can one girl from each pair go to the pantry to collect the ingredients.”

“I’ll go!” Harper jumped to her feet.

While she raced off to get the ingredients, I took the liberty to read the recipe card. It seemed pretty simple, but then, of course, I'd never made cupcakes before. They weren’t allowed in my house, ever! Mom used to grab my arm and drag me past any bakeries and cafes before I had a chance to study their window displays properly. I stared open-mouthed at the recipe card; wow, that was a lot of sugar. My mom wouldn't allow me to eat that much sugar in a lifetime!

Harper lugged over a wooden crate, it was full of white looking ingredients, well, all except the eggs. I licked my lips, eager to get started. I'd never baked cakes before, and I was looking forward to it (not that I was going to tell Harper that.)

Ms. Ekelby had already preheated the ovens, which meant that we could jump straight to the second instruction on the recipe card. We stuck the butter into the mixing bowl, and Harper cracked the eggs into it. I laughed as I fished out the bits of eggshell that had fallen in. I went to grab the sugar and was about to pour it in when Harper leaned in close to me.

"I switched the sugar for salt," Harper whispered. "How dare a teacher talk to me like that. This will show her!" She smirked.

I shrugged, guessing it could be kind of funny. I'd just have to make sure I ate some of the other groups' cupcakes and not ours.

"Let's do it." I managed a smile.

Harper laughed as she tipped in the salt and I found myself laughing too.

"What's so funny?" Taylor looked over at us.

"Oh nothing." Harper smiled.

We all stirred the mixture then scooped it into the cupcake cases. While the cupcakes were cooking, Ms. Elkelby gave us all a frosting demonstration.

"You can decorate them however you want, be creative

girls." She waved the frosting pipe around.

She had a smudge of green icing on her cheek which some of the girls were giggling about.

"I didn't realize that the 'Shrek look' was in," Harper whispered to me.

I held back a laugh, admittedly that was pretty funny. That shade of green icing looked like puke; we definitely weren't using that color.

"We need to ice them differently to everyone else's, so we know which not to eat," Harper whispered.

I nodded in agreement, even though I'd already thought of that.

We took the cupcakes out of the oven, fanned them to cool them down and then began icing. They smelt good, really good. If it hadn't been for the fact that I knew ours were tainted, I would have found it difficult to resist eating one.

"Let's make ours white and purple," Harper suggested.

"That sounds perfect," I said.

I used purple icing to make a twirl shape for the top, while Harper thickly covered our cakes with white icing.

By the end of it, the room was full of cupcakes, Brianna and Taylor's were decorated as rainbows and Amy and Emma's were chocolate frosted with pink sprinkles on top.

Ms. Ekelby walked around the room studying the cupcakes. "These look excellent girls. Now, which should I test?"

"Miss, try one of ours!" Brianna waved her arms about as she jumped up and down.

Oh no, I thought, as I tried to maintain a normal smile. *Please don't pick ours, please don't pick ours.*

I smiled at Miss Ekelby as she studied our cupcakes, she walked off and studied Brianna and Taylor's cupcakes.

"Miss, miss, please try one," Brianna clapped her hands together.

"Okay Brianna, they do look lovely." She hovered her hand over them as she deliberated which to choose. "I think I'll go with this one." She picked one up, peeled back the casing and then took a delicate bite out of it.

Brianna looked at her with puppy dog eyes, eager for appraisal. The teacher finished chewing and then looked at Brianna and Taylor. "Delicious girls."

Brianna giggled excitedly and then hugged Taylor.

"This class has been a great success." She smiled. "Now girls, please put your cupcakes in the freezer so they'll be ready for the dance on Saturday."

At the mention of the D-word, the class erupted into cheers and excited murmurs. I couldn't wait for the dance, especially as it seemed likely that it was going to go with a salty-sweet bang!

Chapter Six - Talking to Boys

It was early morning, and I sat on my bed, amusing myself by scrolling through my phone.

Brianna was jumping around in front of Sydney begging her to give her a boy lesson. I snorted and pretended that I wasn't interested, but really, I secretly was. So okay, when it came to boys I wasn't as clueless as Brianna, but at the same time I'd been stuck in an all-girls boarding schools since I was five, so I hadn't exactly had a lot to do with boys. Sydney, on the other hand, seemed to know her stuff.

I just wanted to get ready in peace, but Brianna had other ideas. She was jumping around in front of me like Tigger so that I was struggling to concentrate on anything else.

"Bree, I need to get ready." I looked around for my pencil case.

"But I don't know how to talk to boys." Brianna moved directly in front of me.

"Look, Bree..." I gripped her shoulders and moved her out of the way. "It's all about being confident and natural."

"But I don't know how to be those things," she sobbed. "I need help! You told me you'd teach me how to deal with boys. So, teach me!!!" she screamed.

The door opened, and Miss Crombie peered in. "Is everything okay?"

Brianna looked at her with a tear-stained face.

"Brianna, what's wrong?"

"Sydney promised to teach me about boys, but now she's holding back. I need more lessons," she sobbed.

We all burst out laughing, including Miss Crombie.

"What do you need to know?" Miss Crombie asked her.

"Everything." Brianna gave an exaggerated sigh. "I need to know how to talk to boys."

"You just need to speak naturally and be confident," Miss Crombie replied with a smile.

To be fair, that was basically my advice. Maybe Miss Crombie wasn't as ancient and unworldly as I'd first thought.

Brianna threw herself back on my bed and gave a loud sigh. "Thank you, Miss Crombie," she huffed.

"Right, well I have places to be and people to speak to. Bye girls." She gave a wave.

I and the others said bye back to her. When Harper was sure that the teacher was out of earshot, she burst out laughing.

Harper walked across the room and looked straight at Taylor. "All you need to do is to speak naturally," she mimicked Miss Crombie's voice. "You just need to speak naturally and be confident."

Both Taylor and I were in hysterics. Brianna remained on my bed; her arms crossed in annoyance.

"But I don't know how to talk to them," Taylor impersonated Brianna. "My life is OVER!" She stood up, flailed her arms about and then collapsed down onto her bed.

"All you need to do is follow my advice, as I'm one-hundred-and-fifty-years-old and am therefore experienced in such matters." Harper tried to hold back her laughter.

"But I don't know what to do," Taylor whined. "I'm terrible with boys, it's a disaster, I'm a disaster. My life is over!" She buried her head in her arms.

I eventually stopped laughing and looked at Brianna, she still had her arms folded and looked glum. I couldn't take this anymore, I realized that I much preferred giggly Brianna to the miserable one.

"Okay, calm down." I looked at Harper and Taylor, they were still laughing like hyenas. "I need a tranquil atmosphere for Brianna's next lesson."

"Really?" Brianna looked at me with wide eyes. "You mean it?" she sniffed.

"Yes Brianna." I rolled my eyes. "Now, come on, I don't have all day."

She gave an enthusiastic nod, and both Harper and Taylor sniggered.

"First of all, you have to be positive, if you think it will go wrong, then it will. Calm your nerves with breathing exercises or by dancing your nervous energy away. When you feel calm, walk straight up to Elliot, making sure you make eye contact."

"Then what?" she asked

"Say something about the dance."

"Like what?" she stared at me.

Jeez, this girl was clueless.

"Talk about the music, the dance, or if you really can't think of anything tell him you like his shoes or something."

"His shoes." She gave me a puzzled look.

"Yes Brianna, his shoes. Or maybe comment on his t-shirt or something instead," I replied.

"What if he isn't wearing a t-shirt?"

"He's hardly going to show up without a top on." My reply was tinged with sarcasm.

"But what if he's wearing a sweater?"

"Then comment on it." I gritted my teeth.

Harper and Taylor were laughing in the background, and I couldn't blame them. Brianna seemed oblivious to this but then that was hardly surprising, that girl may as well have been in her own giant bubble.

"But I don't know how to comment," Brianna whined.

"Okay, so it all depends on the situation. Say for instance that Elliot is at the food table looking at the atrocious cupcakes we made-"

"Our cupcakes weren't atrous-i-ous, they were amazing," she interrupted.

"You could go up to him and say h*ey, what do you think of the cakes we made?"*

"But what if I mess it up?" she asked.

I took a deep breath and tried to remain calm. This was easy, really easy. They were boys, not Martians.

"Harper, can you pretend to be a boy?" I asked in a pleading voice.

Harper smirked but gave a nod in agreement.

"Okay, Bree, pretend that Harper is a really cute boy, go and talk to him."

"I don't just want any old boy, I want Elliot." Brianna whined.

"Well then, pretend that she is Elliot."

"Okay." Brianna stood up, took a deep breath, then stiffly walked over to Harper.

I couldn't contain it anymore, I burst out laughing.

"What?" She turned and glared at me.

"Sorry," I croaked. "Maybe try to lose the robot walk."

At the mention of the word *robot* both Harper and Taylor started laughing, which set me off again. We carried on like that for a few minutes before we all calmed down.

"Can we get on with my lesson now?" Brianna huffed.

"Go ahead," I said.

"Hey Elliot," she almost fell over as she swished her hair back.

Harper started laughing, and Brianna glared at her.

"Do it again," I told Brianna.

"Hey," she smiled at Harper. "What do you think of the cakes we made?" she said in a husky voice.

"You sound like you've swallowed a frog." Taylor chuckled.

Brianna coughed to clear her voice. "Hey Elliot, what do you think of the cakes we made?" she squeaked.

"Now you sound like a mouse!" Harper sniggered.

Both Taylor and Harper had a point, she did sound more like those creatures than herself. I marched over to her and turned her around, so she was facing me.

"Okay Bree, you need to remember to breathe." I gripped her shoulders. "And to speak naturally and to be confident."

"Okay." She gave an excited nod.

"Breath." I demonstrated by breathing in through my nose and then out of my mouth for longer. "Breathe."

Brianna copied my breathing. "Okay, I'm ready." She did her clapping seal thing.

Jeez, was she deliberately trying to impersonate every animal? I walked over to my bed and sat down on the edge of it. Brianna walked across the room, spun around, shook out her arms, took a deep breath and then strode over to Harper, her eyes focused on Harper's face.

"Hey." Brianna smiled at Harper. "What do you think of the cakes we made?"

That was a huge improvement and her walk wasn't bad. She also managed to maintain eye contact and not sound like a loony.

Harper pretended to take a bite out of an imaginary cake then chewed. "Yuck! They taste horrible!"

The was a pause of silence before we all burst out laughing. Brianna didn't join in at first, but our laughter was contagious, so it wasn't long before she joined in with a giggle. Our laughter subsided, and I walked over to my desk and began sorting my books out. When I turned around, my arms full of books, Brianna was standing there like my backward shadow.

"What if he isn't at the food table. How do I start a conversation then?" she asked.

"I don't know." I shrugged, as I put my books down on my bed and began to sort through them.

"Yes, you do know, you know everything when it comes to boys," Brianna replied earnestly.

Harper laughed, and Taylor snorted at this comment, but Brianna ignored them.

"Please Sydney, you said you'd help me," her eyes pleaded with me.

"I have been helping you. I just have to get ready for lessons, and I still can't find my pencil case."

"Please, I just need a few examples of what to say to him," Brianna pleaded. She was down on her knees, looking at me with big puppy dog eyes. This girl was driving me crazy;

she was more annoying than Moaning Myrtle. Whine, whine, whine, whine, whine, she was like a stuck record. Still, I had agreed to help her.

"Okay, so here are some examples: Do you like this song? Hi, I haven't seen you around before, my name's Brianna, what's yours? Welcome to our school, are you enjoying the dance?"

"Stop! I'm getting confused." She rubbed her head. "I'll learn those ones, for now, thank you."

She skipped off and left me to try and find my pencil case. A minute later she came back and held out my sparkly pink pencil case, a broad smile on her face.

"Where did you find that?" I took it off her.

"Taylor's desk," she sang out.

I scowled over at Taylor.

"I forgot I borrowed it." She blushed. "Sorry."

"Whatever, at least I have it now. Thanks, Bree," I smiled at her.

"No problem. And thank you for helping me, I mean, I know I can go on and stuff, but I just want to be clear on everything. You're so confident, and I'm so not…" she sighed.

"Look, you're a fun girl. All you need to do is remember to relax, and you'll ace it."

"I guess." Brianna gave a thoughtful look. "Thanks, Sydney, you're the best."

I transferred my textbooks back onto my desk and placed my pencil case on top of them. I took one last look to check everything was in order before I followed the others out of the room, and we made our way to breakfast.

"Hey, boy expert," Harper smirked, as she sidled up to me.

"Compared to Brianna I am a boy genius." I grinned.

"I so hope Elliot eats one of our cupcakes in front of her, that would be hilarious." Harper giggled and I joined her.

"Yeah." I bit down on my lip. "That would be hilarious!"

I looked at Brianna as she giggled at something Taylor had said and then she clapped like a seal. Yeah, she was annoying, but she didn't deserve to be humiliated. I hoped for her sake that if she did talk to Elliot at the cupcake table, that he wouldn't pick up one of ours.

Chapter Seven - Miss Alanke is Mean!

I like 'girl world' being peaceful and all, but that didn't mean that there wasn't room for the occasional practical joke. After all, this decrepit old place did need livening up now and again.

History was my least favorite lesson. This was mainly because our teacher, Miss Alanke, she's super mean. She was sourer than a lemon, in fact, I doubted she ever smiled in her life unless it was at the expense of someone else. That's why I decided that the best place for a practical joke was in one of her mundane classes.

She always played an inspiring (otherwise known as ridiculously boring) video clip at the start of each class. The last one was of a bunch of geese flying and was meant to emphasize the importance of working together or something stupid like that. I hated those videos, and so did all of the other girls. They were pointless and a complete waste of time, yet Miss Alanke played them religiously. I imagined her sitting at home each night, clicking away at her laptop as she scrolled the internet for more of these videos to bore her victims with.

I wolfed down my breakfast extra quickly and made some excuse about needing to visit the library. Instead, I made my way along the maze-like corridors and sneaked into the classroom. It was a boring cream painted room, there wasn't as much as one poster adorning the wall. Apparently, posters meant clutter and Miss Alkane had no time for that.

I sat down at her desk and checked her laptop. Unsurprisingly, she had no password protecting it, like seriously, what was with old people and technology? The morning video was there, all ready to bore its watchers. I turned down the volume before I clicked play and some cartoon monkeys appeared on the screen. I rolled my eyes before I clicked the pause button.

It was sabotaging time. I thought, a devious smile on my face.

Fifteen-minutes later I walked back into the classroom, Miss Alkane was standing by the door so she could inspect our uniforms. As soon as everyone crossed into her domain, they fell silent as if they were entering a dragon's lair. I could feel her stern eyes on me, but she didn't say anything, after all, I was dressed immaculately.

"Amy, tuck your blouse in more, this is a school, not a youth club," she said through pursed lips.

Amy quickly stuffed her blouse further into her skirt, a terrified look on her face. I walked across the room and sat down next to Brianna, who wasn't giggly for once. Even she knew better than to provoke Miss Alkane's wraith.

"Grace, tie your hair up properly, those straggly bits at the front are not school policy," she said sternly to her.

Grace gave a nod before she immediately redid her hair, making sure there were no loose strands. I smiled to myself, I found it amusing how one old woman could insight so much fear into everyone. Seriously, she should have been a judge or something, not a history teacher in some posh school.

As she walked to the front of the class, only the clacking of her sensible black heels could be heard.

"Today's video is very inspiring and will hopefully influence you to all to create this type of future for yourselves," she announced.

I clamped my teeth down on my gums to stop myself from laughing-out-loud. Unbeknown to her she'd just given the perfect introduction to what was going to be a not-so-perfect video. She clicked play, and instead of looking down at the screen she stared at the girls, gauging their reactions. This was usually the part that we all struggled with. If we so much as flinched during one of her videos, she would glare at us. Looking away from the screen, even for a second caused her to wag a stern finger at us. If we dared to yawn during one, then we ended up with detention.

At first, there was an audible gasp, then all the girls burst out laughing. Miss Alanke's eyes widened in alarm. She didn't know who to scold first, or why everyone was being so disrespectful in her class. How dare they laugh at one of her inspiring videos. That's when she turned and looked at the whiteboard which the video was being projected onto. Bikini wearing cheerleaders were parading along a beach with red and white pompoms. Miss Alanke let out an ear-piercing scream which only caused the girls to laugh more. She ran up to the screen and tried to cover the images with her arms.

I can only put her stupidity down to shock. I mean, why else would she try to cover the projected images instead of just walking over to her laptop and pressing stop? Like, duh!

Everyone was howling with laughter, Brianna and a few of the other girls had jumped up onto their chairs and were copying the cheerleading moves. I remained in my seat and laughed silently to myself.

My prank had gone far better than I ever could have imagined. This was indeed one way to liven up a boring history class.

The door swung open, and in walked Miss Braun, she saw Miss Alanke desperately trying to cover the projected video. With a frown, she walked over to the laptop and paused the video, right as one of the cheerleaders was bent over and wriggling her bottom. This caused the girls to burst into fresh fits of laughter, even the menacing principal's glare couldn't contain their laughter. Although, Brianna and the others had hopped down from their chairs as soon as she'd entered the room.

Miss Braun closed the laptop lid, causing the image to vanish off the screen. The laughing subsided and the focus changed to Miss Alanke, who was still trying to cover the whiteboard with her arms.

"So, Miss Alanke, before you started the daily inspirational video you said that it would influence us to create this type of future for ourselves. Does that mean that you want us all to aspire to become cheerleaders and wear tiny bikinis?" Harper obviously couldn't resist rubbing it in.

Miss Alanke's face turned beetroot red. It was then that she realized that she was still trying to cover a blank screen, so she quickly lowered her arms. I'd never seen the usually scary teacher speechless before, it was as though someone had drained all of her power away.

Unfortunately for Harper, Miss Braun wasn't in a state of shocked delirium. "Leave the classroom immediately," she glared at Harper.

Harper knew better than to try and question this, but she failed to hide her smile as she walked out of the room.

"Settle down right this instance!" Miss Braun stared at the rest of us. "If you don't then I won't hesitate to cancel the school dance."

If ever there was a statement that could inject the fear into everyone, well, it was that. The laughter stopped promptly. Miss Braun gave a satisfied nod before she walked over to Miss Alanke. "Here, sit down," she guided her over to her chair.

Miss Alanke opened her mouth to reply, but only a gurgling sound came out that sounded like someone was drowning in their own spit.

We all struggled not to laugh at this, but the fear of the dance being canceled was enough to make us all hold back.

"Dear, sip this," Miss Braun picked up the glass of water that was on Miss Alanke's desk and passed it to her.

She gave a nod as she took a couple of small sips. "Thank you," she croaked. "I'll take it from here."

Miss Braun gave a nod, before she glared at us all as she walked across the room. As soon as she stepped outside of the classroom, she began yelling at Harper to go to her office. It seemed as though it sucked to be Harper, when would she learn that sometimes *silence was golden*?

The rest of the lesson went by in a blur. I'm sure that no one was concentrating on what Miss Alanke was dithering on about and the shock had caused her to lack her usual sternness. I found myself daydreaming about Harper and what Miss Braun was saying to her in her office. She must have thought that Harper had switched the videos, if this were the case then Harper would be in big trouble! Oh well, that was her problem, not mine. I wasn't going to say anything to make anyone think any different.

One thing was for sure, if all of the lessons were this amusing, then this place wouldn't have been so bad.

Harper

Miss Braun thought I was responsible for the video prank. It didn't matter how much I protested my innocence; her mind was clearly set. It was so unfair because I didn't do it. Could she really blame me for commenting like I did? I mean hello, the whole scenario was hilarious. This didn't mean that I did it though. She was being unfair by blaming me without any proof. Worse still, she rang up my mom and told her what I'd *allegedly* done. My mom was so mad that she said to me that if I got into trouble again that term, then I wouldn't be going home for the holidays. That was probably just an excuse for her and my dad to go off on an expensive holiday without me.

This whole situation was super unfair, I wasn't behind the stupid video prank. Even I knew better than to mess with Miss Alanke's inspirational videos. Although, the fearsome teacher had looked pitiful.

"Miss, I didn't do it. You should call the police and get them to run fingerprint tests on Miss Alanke's laptop, then you'll see that I never touched it. It wasn't me; it wasn't."

"Then who do you assume it was?" Miss Braun raised an eyebrow at me.

"I don't know, but it wasn't me," I protested. "Blaming me without any proof is really unfair. Do a lie detector test, and then you'll see that it wasn't me. It really wasn't Miss, do a test, and then you'll see that it wasn't me."

"May I remind you that it was your choice to make that unnecessary remark." She gave me a stern look.

"I know Miss, and that was immature of me. I'm sorry, I truly am, but it honestly wasn't me who was responsible for the video prank." I gave my best innocent look.

"Taking delight in others misery isn't what St Andrew's girls should do." She continued to scowl at me. "As if Miss Alanke wasn't traumatized enough."

"I know Miss, I shouldn't have done it. I don't know what came over me, but I can assure you that I won't make a comment like that again."

There was a silent pause which seemed to go on for ages. Miss Braun was at her most frightening when she was silent, as who knew what thoughts were rotating in her mind.

"I could choose to exclude you from the dance as punishment."

I gasped, she couldn't do that, could she? My life would be over if I missed the dance.

She gave a deep sigh and then repositioned the thin gold chain that she wore around her wrinkled neck. "On this occasion, I won't ban you from the dance. But if I find out that you were in any way responsible for the videos being switched then not only will you be excluded from the dance; you will also face a month's worth of detention. Do I make myself clear?"

"Yes Miss, thank you Miss."

"Okay then. I suggest you leave my office promptly before I change my mind."

She didn't need to tell me twice! I smiled at her before I quick-walked out of her office. Now, that was a close call. In future, I needed to learn to bite my tongue and hold onto my sarcastic remarks, however much I yearned to say them.

***

I walked into art class (another utterly pointless subject), and immediately everyone stopped mid-paint and gawped at me. I wanted to tell them all to get a life, but instead, I gave them my best smile. My eyes stayed on Sydney; she was smirking at me. That's when I knew that she'd been behind the video prank. Of course, she'd left breakfast early with some nonsense about needing to go to the library.

Miss Finnigan smiled over at me; her arms splattered with splodges of wet paint. "Ah Harper, you've joined us. We're carrying on with our watercolor paintings."

I nodded in response before I sat down next to Sydney. I deliberated how to play this. Should I pretend that I did the video prank to gage her reaction? Should I pretend that I'm being kicked out of school to see if she would confess? Or should I just tell her exactly what went down in Miss Braun's office and see if she felt guilty? Nah, she would have taken too much delight out of that. Instead, I decided to play it cool and see if she confessed after class.

"I'm glad you're back." Sydney gave me a sickly-sweet smile.

"Me too." I grabbed a paintbrush.

I sensed how eager she was to ask me what'd happened. She must have decided that class wasn't the place to talk about it. I feigned interest in my stupid picture, grateful that I had the rest of the lesson to work out what I was going to say. There was no way that I was letting Sydney get one up on me; no chance!

***

Lunchtime arrived, and naturally, I was the hot topic. I marched over to my table, my tray in hand and pretended not to notice their eyes on me as I cut up a piece of potato and popped it into my mouth.

"So, what happened?" Brianna stared at me with eager eyes.

I purposely chewed extra slowly. "Not much." I shrugged.

"But you were in there for ages," Amy said.

"Me and Miss Braun were having a catch-up tea and cake." I smirked at her. I could tell that she wasn't sure if I was being serious or not. That girl was super dumb and annoying.

"So, you're not in trouble?" Brianna asked.

"Nah, although I set up the video." I looked directly at Sydney as I said it, but her expression didn't falter. "But with my connections I'm untouchable."

"Are you still allowed to go to the dance?" Brianna asked.

Everyone else seemed to lean in further to hear my response. Apparently, this had been the gossip that had spread like wild fire around the school.

"The dance would be nothing without me, and you all know it," I replied. Sure, I sounded big-headed, but it was true. The dance would have been a complete flop without me there. As far as they knew I'd got away unpunished from doing the video prank and traumatizing Miss Alanke. Which only meant that I was further cementing my position as the alpha girl in this place.

Everyone was looking at me and hanging on my every word. I was the leader, and they all knew it. I was untouchable.

"I'm glad you'll be there Harper." Brianna giggled as she smiled at me.

"Thanks, Bree."

"Me too." Sydney gave me a half smile.

I smiled back at her, my eyes locking with hers. She knew that I knew it was her who'd switched the videos. She was the princess of pranks (I was the queen), so of course, it'd been her. No one else was that smart or daring. I had to admit that I liked her style, but she was no match for me.

Harper was smart, but she wasn't as smart as me. I knew when to bite my lip and sit back and watch my plan unfold, but sometimes she couldn't resist the urge to dive straight in. That's why she'd ended up in Miss Braun's office and had no doubt been threatened with endless detentions and a dance ban.

We currently had a stare-off, neither of us prepared to be the first to look away. I kept on looking at her as I put a forkful of chicken into my mouth and chewed on it. I wasn't surprised that she'd managed to talk her way out of trouble as that was what Harper did best.

She knew that the video prank had been me and I knew that

she knew this. Neither of us was going to admit this to the other, but we both knew and that's what this stare-off was about. Brianna dropped her spoon into her bowl and bits of custard shot out and splattered Harper on the arm. She jerked back, in doing so she broke eye contact with me.

She gave Brianna a dirty look as she wiped the custard off her arm.

"Sorry," Brianna said coyly.

I won the stare-off, but then I was always going to…regardless of Brianna and her clumsiness. Harper was good, but she was no match for me.

Chapter Eight - The Dance

After the longest week ever Saturday arrived, FINALLY!!! Better still, Miss Braun let us have the morning off lessons so that we could prepare ourselves. Maybe she wasn't such a witch after all. Nah, scrap that, she was definitely a witch, all she needed was a broom and a black cat, and she'd be Halloween ready.

I went for a walk to my secret spot on the school grounds, mainly just so I could have a break from Brianna's whining. That girl was driving me mad with her drama queen antics about boys. I almost felt sorry for Sydney having to deal with her…almost.

I arrived back at the room to find Brianna having a meltdown because Sydney wouldn't let her borrow one of her outfits. I contemplated grabbing my stuff and going into Tiff's room to get ready, but I decided against it. Brianna was annoying, but this was like my own personal live soap-opera. I grabbed my makeup case, then I sat down on my bed and rifled through it.

Okay, so Sydney had some coolish clothes, but mine was better. Still, I didn't blame her for telling Brianna she couldn't borrow an outfit, that girl was far too excitable and clumsy to wear something nice.

Brianna was driving me INSANE!!! Even though I'd had all day to get ready, I'd barely made a start, and that was down to her and her constant indecisiveness. Now she had to cheek to try and borrow one of my very expensive outfits.

"Bree, I need to get ready," I said sternly.

"Please, please, please let me wear your pink sparkly dress. Please, please, please?" She pressed her hands together and looked at me all doe-eyed.

"No," I said assertively, as I passed her and then leaned over to grab my hairbrush off my bedside table.

"What about the green skirt then?" she moved as close to me

as she could, so I barely had the arm room to move my brush through my hair.

"You totally couldn't pull that skirt off," Harper piped in.

"I so could." Brianna's bottom lip began to shake.

Great, just what I needed, waterworks!!! Thanks a lot, Harper. "Stop!" I put down my hairbrush and gripped her shoulders. "You have loads of nice outfits, wear one of those."

"I don't want to wear a nice outfit, I want to wear an amazing one," she sobbed. "I'm so nervous about talking to Elliot, I don't want to mess it up. I keep forgetting my breathing exercises and what you told me to say to him. On top of all this, I have to wear one of my boring outfits, and he's never going to like me in one of those."

"Brianna, calm down!" I gently shook her. "You will be fine, okay?"

"No, because I will look stupid."

"She has a point." Harper sniggered.

This caused a fresh bout of tears to stream down Brianna's cheeks. Thanks again, Harper…NOT!

I looked over at Taylor, she was already in her floral print cream dress, and she had nearly finished plaiting a cute braid in her hair. If I didn't do something to shut Brianna up, then I would be going to the dance in my sweatpants…shudder!

I walked over to Brianna's bed and looked down at her collection of clothes that she'd laid out.

"What about this one?" I picked up a pale blue dress with

pink sparkle on it that matched the pink sash.

"I look like a 7-year-old in it." She folded her arms in protest.

"It *is* a bit babyish," Harper remarked, as she applied mascara.

I secretly hoped that she'd stab herself in the eye with the mascara wand.

"I have nothing to wear," Brianna swiped her clothes off her bed and then slumped down onto it, face first. "Fine, I just won't go. I hate my life, I hate it!" She thudded her fists into her bedcover.

"Fine!" I shouted. "You can borrow something."

She instantly stopped sobbing, sat up and looked at me. "Really, you mean it?" She sniffed as she rubbed her eyes.

"Yes, but I get to pick what it is," I said, sounding like my mother.

Brianna nodded enthusiastically.

"And the deal is you let me get ready in peace," I demanded.

She was about to reply, but I spoke before she could.

"I mean it Bree, no more annoying me."

"Okay." She gave a less enthusiastic nod this time.

"I walked over to the only wardrobe in the room which I had to share with the other girls. My party clothes stood out from the rest of the plain things hanging up. I ran my fingers over the material, deliberating which to lend her. My hands stopped on a little black dress, and she looked from the black dress to me, her eyes pleading. *No chance*. That dress was mine and mine alone. Besides, it wasn't a very Brianna type dress. That dress screamed sophisticated while she was giggly and hyperactive.

I took out a cute dark orange checked skirt and held it out to her. "Here, take it."

"Thank you, I love it," she squealed.

"If you get a mark on it then you're paying for it to be dry cleaned," I demanded in a stern voice.

She gave a nod, but I wasn't even sure if she'd heard me correctly, as she was excitedly looking at the skirt.

"Right, now I'm going to get ready in peace."

Harper snorted. She had finished her makeup and was now finalizing her outfit. It wasn't fair that she hadn't had to put up with Brianna whinging at her. I smirked as an idea popped into my head.

I looked over at Bree, who had already put on my clothes and was now parading up-and-down the room in it.

"Bree, you look great, but I think you're missing something," I said.

"What?" She immediately stopped walking and stared at me.

"Oh, it doesn't matter," I looked down at my blue nails (which I'd painted earlier.)

"What is it?" She bounced over to me.

"I mean you look great and all…but it's a shame you haven't got the makeup to complete the look."

"But I'm no good at applying makeup." She gave me a downcast look.

"Harper is, I'm sure she'll help you, won't you Harper?" I said, trying to hold back a smile.

"I'm busy," she said through gritted teeth.

Brianna hurried over to Harper, she put her hands together and gave her the doe-eyed treatment. "Please Harper, please, please, please, please, please help me."

"I'm busy, ask Taylor." Harper was doing her best to totally ignore her.

Taylor gave a stunned look.

"But Taylor can't apply makeup like you can."

"I'm busy," Harper growled.

Brianna stood directly in front of her so that she struggled to do anything. When Harper made the slightest of movements, Brianna moved too, and she continued to look at her with pleading eyes. After a few minutes of this Harper relented.

"Fine," she huffed. "Sit down on my bed."

"Thank you, thank you, thank you. You're amazing, I'm so happy, thank you, thank you, thank you." Brianna clapped her hands together.

Harper gave me a disgruntled look, and I smirked back at her. Finally, I could get ready in peace.

I put my hair into cute buns, applied a thin layer of makeup and the subtle look was super sophisticated and I finished off my look with a layer of my favorite apple-flavored lip gloss; fruity! I changed into my outfit, sprayed myself with my flower blossom body mist and then barged the other girls out of the way so I could study myself in the mirror. I could feel their envious eyes fixed on me, I looked good, and they all knew it. Harper and Brianna may have had their sights set on Elliot, but he was going to be mine, not theirs.

Thanks to Sydney I was behind on my getting-ready routine. My makeup was expensive, and I didn't want to share it with anyone. Brianna wasn't even bothered about makeup, and she would have stayed that way if Sydney hadn't mentioned it. It seemed easier to just stick some makeup on her to silence her, so, I put some glittery silver eyeshadow on and gave her a coat of pink-tinted lip gloss.

After that she left me in peace, well, if you could call her prancing up-and-down in front of the mirror and practicing what she was going to say to Elliot...peace. She was wasting her time, Brianna was average at best, and a boy like Elliot would never be interested in her.

As for Sydney, I guess she was pretty in a homely kind of way, but she was no match for me. Neither Bree or Syd had my personality and confidence. They were no competition for me! Elliot would be my boyfriend, not theirs, and they'd just have to get used to it.

Why wouldn't Brianna just be quiet? I'd already had to shove her out of the way twice just to look in the mirror. At first, the way she was acting about boys was kind of funny, but now it had lost all of its humor.

"Elliot, hi, my name's Brianna." She flicked out her hair as she looked in the mirror. "What music do you like? Really? Me too. Hey Elliot, it's great to see you tonight." She placed her hand on her hip and turned to the side. "Hey Elliot, do you like the cupcakes? I made the rainbow frosted ones just for you."

It was official, she was driving me insane!!!

"Elliot, I think I love you…do you want to dance?" she pouted.

I picked up a pillow and threw it at her, it hit her in the head. I burst out laughing, and so did Harper and Taylor.

"Ha, ha, very funny." She turned and glared at me. "You've ruined my train of thought, now I'll have to start again."

"No!" Harper screamed. "Besides, if you practice too much your mind will go blank at the dance, and if you pout at Elliot like that, he'll probably run for his life."

"No, he won't," she moaned. "Will he?" she looked at me.

I needed to play this cool, our sanity was at stake.

"Well," I sighed. "I hate to say it but Harper's right. I think it's best if you go and rest or you could end up looking really stupid in front of Elliot...if you over-practice."

Brianna looked worried. She gave a feeble nod and then trudged in silence over to her bed and lay down on it.

I gave Harper a close-lipped smile, and she gave me one back. I welcomed the silence and decided that I was never going to agree to give Brianna boy advice ever again.

Harper

We all arrived at the dance early to help set up. Some of the girls helped Mr. Meuler move around chairs, others helped Miss Crombie blow up balloons. I made a beeline for the cupcake table. Unfortunately, someone had beaten me to display them. Worse still, the frosting had blended together on most of them, so it was virtually impossible to tell them apart.

Sydney walked past me carrying a chair, she took one look at the cupcakes and then gave me a wink and a knowing smirk. Sometimes I wondered if we were related, it was as though we had the same thoughts.

"Harper, these balloons won't inflate themselves." Miss Crombie waved me over.

I rolled my eyes; balloons were so childish. I took one last glance at the cupcakes and made a mental note to take a tiny bite of one first.

After an hour of blowing up balloons and moving chairs to the side of the room, the hall was set up. I thought it was ridiculous that we'd been made to do this in our party clothes. I noticed how Amy's hair was stuck to her sweaty forehead. Luckily for me, I always remained looking beautiful.

"Girls, gather around." Miss Braun ushered us over. "It is of the highest importance that you remember that you are representing St Andrews and therefore your behavior must be exemplary. I expect you all to make the boys feel welcome...but not too welcome."

A lot of the girls giggled at this and Sydney looked at me and rolled her eyes.

Drone, drone, drone, Miss Braun went on. I zoned out and found myself thinking about the dance and seeing Elliot again. I was super excited, tonight was going to go perfectly, I just knew it.

Miss Braun finally said, "The Aquinas' students have arrived, please form two lines as a guard of honor outside the hall." We all began to race forward. "Wait!" she shouted, and we all stopped on the spot. "Remember that you are representatives of the school and these are our guests."

She gave us a look that said we could go, so we all quick-walked our way across the hall. Brianna was the quickest, she half-walked, half-bounced her way across the room and slid into the first line position. The other girls couldn't catch me, not even Sydney. I stood opposite Brianna so that I was in the first position on the second line. Sydney stood next to Brianna and tried to look like she wasn't bothered. It was super important to be at the front of the line, Sydney knew that. We'd be the girls that the boys set their eyes on first and out of Brianna and me, well, there was no contest. They'd all be looking at me.

Brianna was fidgeting on the spot. Clearly, her nerves had got to her.

"Stand still," Sydney hissed at her.

"I can't, I'm too excited and nervous and…it's them!" she called out, pointing at the boys.

I followed her gaze and saw that the boys were walking towards us. Strong posture…check. Hand on hip…check. Confident smile…check. I was boy ready.

The first boy was okay looking, he looked straight at me and grinned. I maintained my smile; I didn't have to look at him again to know that his gaze would still be fixed on me as he walked past. The next few boys were either pimply or shorter than me. Still, I kept my smile as they walked towards me and said *hi* and *I'm good thank you* in the appropriate places.

That's when I saw Elliot walking towards us. Brianna gasped, Sydney took a step forward, so her view wasn't blocked by Brianna. I widened my smile and locked my eyes on him. He turned his head, his eyes locked on mine, he smiled. This was easy, too easy but then what did the other girls expect?

Brianna stepped forward and tapped Elliot on the shoulder. He broke our eye contact to turn around.

"Hi there, I just wanted to say that I hope you have an awesome time at the dance," she oozed confidence. "Talk later." she smiled at him.

"Thanks, um, sure," he mumbled back.

She maintained her smile as she stepped back into her place in line. I could see how much she was struggling to contain her excitement; she was a ball of energy ready to explode. This only angered me more, how dare she talk to Elliot, who did she think she was? I told myself to relax, Brianna wasn't confident or cool, she may have fluked a first encounter with Elliot, but she would mess up the next one. The girl was far too excitable to keep her cool around a boy, especially one as cute as Elliot.

My attention turned to Sydney who was still sticking out of line, she was looking at me with a smirk on her face.

I shook my head and mouthed, 'She's such a pain.'

Sydney nodded and shrugged her shoulders. She mouthed back, 'Yeah, she is.'

The rest of the boys walked past, but none of them caught my eye. Elliot was the best-looking boy, so he deserved the best girl, which was me, of course. I looked over at Brianna who was no longer containing her excitement. Instead, she was panting as she clapped her hands together as she rambled on to an unamused looking Sydney. I rolled my eyes, and Sydney grinned back. Jeez, Brianna was annoying. Why were some people so utterly clueless?

The last of the boys walked into the hall, so we followed them in. Most of the girls raced over to the refreshments table, but I didn't do that. Instead, I confidently walked over to the opposite side of the room to where the boys were sitting and took a seat. Sydney sat down next to me, a smirk still on her face.

"So, who's your favorite boy?" she asked.

I raised an eyebrow, knowing full well that she knew it was Elliot.

"I'm not sure I like any of them," I replied.

"There must be one that's caught your eye?"

"I suppose there are a few okay ones, beats looking at all of your ugly faces, anyway. Who do you have your eye on?"

She stared to where the majority of the boys were sitting. Many of them had grabbed a drink and cake on their way in.

"I wonder if any of them have our cupcakes?" Sydney grinned.

I chuckled. "So, who?" I was determined to not let Sydney change the subject.

She shrugged and replied, "Time will tell."

Time will tell, what kind of a stupid answer was that? I saw how she looked at Elliot, so I knew it was him that she liked. She was just going to have to deal with the fact that he was going to be mine, not hers.

Brianna bounced her way over to us, her mouth full of cupcake.

"He's so dreamy," she took another bite of cake and chewed. "Did you see how he looked at me? He likes me, I just know it. This is going to be the best dance EVER!"

I exchanged a knowing look with Sydney. Brianna took annoying to a whole new level, we all deserved medals just for putting up with her.

So, the DJ wasn't bad at all, so far, he'd played a One Direction tune and a Taylor Swift song. Miss Braun had done an excellent job there. It was just a shame that no one was dancing. Instead, the girls and boys were giving each other awkward glances like they were both alien species. It was embarrassing really, but I wasn't going to be the first to dance, that would look far too eager. Besides, Elliot was going to ask me to dance soon; I just knew it.

"I want to dance," Brianna announced.

"Not yet." I glared back at her.

"But I'm bored." She was tapping her feet and moving around in her seat.

"Not yet," I repeated.

"Fine." She straightened her shoulders. "Here goes."

I watched in dismay as she strutted her way over to Elliot's group. When I had composed myself from the shock of her boldness, I stood up and did a calm and relaxed walk over there. There was no chance I was letting her ruin things between Elliot and me, no way!

When I got there Brianna was using Sydney's practice lines on Elliot…cringe! He looked at me (probably because he wanted me to save him) and I felt a strong connection between us. The latest Ariana Grande song started playing, and I gave a sly smile, this was a perfect song for Elliot and me to dance to.

"Oooh, I love this song," Brianna grinned at Elliot.

"Yeah, I guess it's okay," he muttered.

He clearly didn't like her and was just being nice. Why couldn't she bounce off and annoy someone else? How could she be so oblivious to how ridiculous she was being? A boy as cute as Elliot would never like a girl as plain as her.

I coughed to clear my throat and looked straight at him.

"Hi." He smiled at me before he turned back to look at Brianna. "Um, would you like to dance?" he asked Brianna.

WHAT!!! Why did he ask plain Jane to dance? Why didn't he ask me? I looked up at the high arched ceiling and willed for the aliens to come and teleport me into space.

Brianna let out an excited giggle and gave a nod. He took her hand and led her over to the dancefloor. He was meant to be holding my hand, not hers! I stared at them open-mouthed, I was too shocked to try and keep my cool. How could this have happened? I was everything Brianna wasn't, so why was he dancing with her and NOT me!!!

The rest of Elliot's group were talking to me, but I didn't care what they had to say. Instead, I kept on glancing over at Elliot and Brianna as they danced with each other. On seeing them dancing, more-and-more kids joined them on the dancefloor. I wanted to dance with Elliot, I wanted everyone to stare at me. This was so unfair!!!

"Hey." Sydney sidled up next to me and watched the dancing couple.

"Hi," I muttered back, my eyes not faltering from Elliot and Brianna. "I don't understand it, I, um, I just don't get it."

"Who knows." Sydney shrugged. "Although I am obviously the best teacher." She smirked.

Sydney was right, this was all her fault. Her lame lessons had given Brianna a false sense of confidence. Brianna was a loser though, so I just had to leave her to ruin it for herself. She was bound to stand on his feet or fall over soon enough, and then Elliot would be mine.

Sydney looked away from the dancefloor and smiled at

Elliot's friends. She was all head-tilting and wide-eyed smiles, but I found it hard to feign interest in anything other than Elliot and Brianna. I forced myself to look away from them and try and engage myself in the conversation. I had no idea what they were talking about, nor did I care. I kept on smiling while my mind remained fixed on the fact that the boy I liked was dancing with a loser.

I felt a tap on my shoulder, I turned to see a cute dark-haired boy called Logan smiling at me. I smiled back and flicked my hair behind my back. He was good-looking in a Prince Charming way, and I knew that Amy had a massive crush on him.

"Hi Harper, you look beautiful today," he said.

"Only today?" I gave him a questioning look and a sly smile.

"Today, tomorrow, always," he replied with a confident grin.

"Thanks," I smiled.

"Do you want to dance?" he asked.

"Okay," I replied.

He took my hand and led me onto the dancefloor. I couldn't help but look over at Amy who was sitting with Zoe, Ruby, and Emma. She was looking at us with a hurt look. Emma rubbed her shoulder and said something to her. Like seriously, she needed to get over it...Amy hadn't even spoken to Logan. Besides, she could have him. I'd only agreed to dance with him to get closer to Elliot. When Elliot came to his senses and asked me to dance, then Amy was welcome to Logan. As for Brianna, she was more suited to one of the pimply short boys. She needed to learn her place.

Logan was trying to lead me to the other end of the

dancefloor, so I yanked his hand and pulled him to a more central position, (which also happened to be next to Elliot and Brianna.) We danced, I could feel Logan's eyes on me, but I couldn't stop glancing at Elliot. Worse still, it turns out that Brianna's clumsiness didn't translate to her dancing. She actually had rhythm.

I looked over at Sydney, who was talking with Elliot's friends. She caught my eye and gave a brief wave. I forced a smile back at her before I took a step closer toward Logan and continued to dance.

Seriously, this song never seemed to end. I was sick of having to look like I was enjoying dancing with Logan. Finally, the song finished, I stopped dancing and looked at Elliot and Brianna. She had a stupidly big grin on her face, and I wanted to wipe it off so badly.

"Let's swap partners for the next song," I suggested.

Brianna's smile instantly faded. "I said I'd show Elliot the food table, so he can try one of the delicious cupcakes we made."

I watched on annoyed as they walked off the dancefloor and over to the food table. The next song started, and Logan held out his hand so that he could spin me around. I danced next to him, a forced smile on my face. He was super good looking and the captain of the basketball team, but he wasn't my focus. I wanted Elliot, not him.

I leaned in closer to him so I could speak into his ear. "We should go and check out the food table too, before Brianna eats everything."

"Sure," Logan replied, smiling. "I love cupcakes, especially if they were made by you."

Logan was flirting with me, I mean, I couldn't blame him. I smiled back even though my jaw was hurting. He took my hand, and I tried my best not to flinch it away. We walked side-by-side over to the food table. I felt envious eyes fixed on us (especially Amy's), but I didn't care.

Elliot and Brianna looked like they were getting on great, so great in fact that neither of them seemed to notice us. This was not going well.

"Which did you make, I'd love to try one?" Logan gestured to the cupcakes.

Yeah, he definitely wouldn't have wanted to try one of mine.

"Um, this one." I grabbed the closest one to me and passed it to him.

"It looks great, you're really talented."

"Thanks," I muttered. Elliot had told a joke and Brianna was giggling.

"This is so good," Logan said enthusiastically.

"Huh?"

"The cake," he held it up. "It's the best cupcake I've ever had."

"Um thanks," I looked from him to Elliot.

Why was he looking at her like he liked her? She was giggling like an idiot, how could he possibly like someone that annoying? I felt like I'd been transported into a parallel universe, one where the loser girls got the cute boys. I closed my eyes tightly and willed for things to return to normality. I opened them to find that Sydney had appeared…great! She smiled at me and gave me the okay symbol. I gave a nod of my head in reply. I watched as she walked over to Elliot and started talking to him. Brianna looked furious, but this didn't stop Sydney. I didn't know if I was impressed or annoyed.

I grabbed a cupcake to give me something to take my mind off the disaster that was tonight (I hoped it wasn't one we'd made.) I took a tiny bite...I was safe! I took a bigger bite and nodded in response to whatever Logan was going on about.

Harper was coming across desperate, and it wasn't good. Me on the other hand, well, I was keeping my cool. So, Elliot was being nice to Brianna, that just showed how sweet a guy he was. But it was apparent there was only so much giggling and clapping like a seal antics he could take before he tired of her. Harper was taking it all too seriously, Brianna was no threat.

That Logan boy seemed to like her; he couldn't stop looking at her. Typical Harper, no boy was ever good enough for her. Instead, she wanted the one that she was never going to have.

"What do you think of the dance?" I asked Elliot.

Brianna sulked next to me. I didn't feel bad about it, she'd had plenty of time with Elliot, now it was my turn.

"Yeah, it's great," he smiled.

"I know, right," I put my hand on my hip.

He reached over and took a cupcake. He peeled back the case and took a huge bite out of it. He coughed and spat his mouthful out all over Brianna. She screamed out and jumped back, but bits of chewed up cake was all over her arms and my top (luckily none of it had got on my skirt.)

Harper, Logan and I all burst out laughing. The look on Brianna's face was priceless, she just stood there covered in soggy cake bits and was too shocked to do anything. Elliot gave her an apologetic look before he ran for the door that led out onto the patio. Harper didn't hesitate in racing after him.

I passed Brianna a bunch of napkins, she took them from me and cleaned up her arms and wiped the bits off my top.

"I don't understand," Brianna said. The color had drained from her face. "We were getting on so well, then…bleurgh."

"Maybe he doesn't like cupcakes?" I smirked.

"But everyone likes cupcakes," she whispered.

Logan looked down hesitantly at the uneaten cupcake in his hand before he placed it back on the table, gave us a nod, then walked back over to his friends.

"Come on," I placed my arm around Brianna's shoulders. "Let's go and see if Elliot is okay."

We stepped outside to find Harper gently wiping Elliot's face with a tissue. It was like some soppy scene straight out of a teen romance film. Brianna took one look at them and burst into tears.

"I'm so sorry," she sobbed. "Are you okay?"

"I'm fine, Brianna, but that cake was disgusting," he replied.

Brianna's tears turned into laughter too, and the smile soon returned to her face. Harper and I looked from Elliot to Brianna and then at each other. There seemed to be some chemistry going on between them, and we could both sense it.

"I'm sorry I spat cake all over you," Elliot said, which caused a new round of laughter between them. "Shall we go and get something to drink?"

Brianna gave an eager nod. Elliot took her hand, and they walked back inside. Harper and I exchanged shocked looks before we followed them. Amy was pouring herself a drink when she looked up and saw Harper. She gave her a dirty look.

"What?" Harper glared at her.

"Nothing," she blushed before she scurried off.

"What was that about?" Elliot asked.

"Amy likes Logan, so she doesn't like the fact that Harper was flirting with him," Brianna remarked.

"Oh," he replied.

Harper was struggling to maintain her smile. She looked like she was close to bubbling over like a gone wrong science experiment. I tried to hide my delight at this. Obviously, I wasn't thrilled that Brianna and Elliot were getting on so well, but watching Harper struggle to conceal her annoyance was funny.

"Sydney, can you please pour Elliot a drink?" Brianna asked me.

Why couldn't she pour him one himself? That's when I saw that they were standing really close so that they could hold hands without being spotted doing so by the teachers.

"Sure." I forced a smile.

I poured him a drink and passed it to him.

"Thanks." He smiled, as he took it from me.

His attention turned back to Brianna, and I felt jealousy rage inside of me. All I'd tried to do was help Brianna, and this was the thanks I got in return. There were plenty of boys here, why did she have to like him? I thought back to my last school and how this plain and boring girl called Remmy managed to get the boy I wanted. It couldn't happen again, it just couldn't.

They both gave each other soppy looks before they walked hand-in-hand over to the dancefloor. Harper and I were left there with shocked looks on our faces.

"This has to stop!" Harper announced before she turned her attention to the drinks table.

I watched her pour a drink and then carry it towards the entrance. I shrugged before I stepped onto the dancefloor. Yes, I was going to dance alone, but it was a school dance, so I was going to dance even if it wasn't with Elliot. Before I was entirely on the dancefloor, a nice-looking boy came over to me. He started dancing, so I did too. Dancing with another boy was an excellent way to make Elliot jealous. Also, it just so happened that I was a fantastic dancer.

I discreetly danced my way closer to Elliot, the boy moved with me, clueless to what I was doing. Elliot was staring at me, he looked impressed.

"Where did you learn to dance like that?" He leaned in to ask me.

"I'm a natural," I lied. I didn't need to tell him about the years of dancing lessons that Mom had insisted were essential for a young lady.

"I don't believe you." Elliot raised an eyebrow. "You're too good."

My heart thudded away in my chest; Elliot was definitely the boy for me. The song finished and the next one came on. It was a dud! Almost everyone swarmed off the dancefloor. We all walked over to the drinks table where Harper was standing, holding two full paper cups.

"Here." She smiled, as she passed them to Elliot and Brianna.

She filled two more and passed them to the boy I'd been dancing with and me. As she poured herself a drink, I gave her a suspicious look. Harper definitely wasn't the willing waitress kind of girl.

"The dance is great, isn't it, Sydney?" Harper looked at me before she took a sip from her drink.

"Yeah, it is," I replied.

Harper was definitely up to something; I just didn't know what it was yet.

"What about you, Bree?" Harper looked at her.

Brianna swayed from one-foot-to-another and then hiccupped. She took a large gulp of her drink and then giggled.

"T-the dance is t-the b-best," she slurred.

I narrowed my eyes. I knew that Brianna was far from normal, but something wasn't right with her.

Brianna took another sip of her drink, the color seemed to drain from her face, and she swayed on the spot.

"Brianna, are you okay?" Elliot gave her a worried look.

"No," she replied before she projectile vomited bits of cake and juice all over him. Everyone else immediately jumped back, except for Elliot who stepped forward and caught Brianna as she fell forward.

Teachers came running over from all directions and leaned over Brianna.

"Call an ambulance," Miss Braun yelled at a started looking Miss Elkelby.

She took her mobile out of her pocket as she tottered off out onto the patio area. The emergency bell rang out, and we were all evacuated from the hall.

"Can all Aquinas students please make their way to the bus," a teacher shouted.

The boy I'd been dancing with waved at me before he walked off towards the bus. Elliot didn't say anything; he was clearly in shock and still covered in Brianna's puke. Harper and I watched him talk to a teacher before he was led out by them to the bus. He didn't look back at me, but then I guess he had just been through a traumatic experience.

"Girls, please go to your rooms, the dance is over!" Miss Crombie started herding us up.

The girls moaned and groaned, but they didn't argue with

her. We all begrudgingly trudged back to our rooms.

So, after the grand total of forty-minutes, the dance was over. Thanks a lot, Brianna!!!

Harper

They didn’t need to end the dance, Brianna was fine, she’d just had a little bit too much to drink. Okay, so I hadn’t meant for her to pass out or anything, I’d just wanted her to make a fool of herself, so I'd added some vodka to her orange squash. It was her own fault; she shouldn’t have gone after Elliot.

Brianna didn't return that night, but Miss Crombie assured us that she'd be fine. The next morning before we left for church, Miss Crombie came into our room to give us the latest Brianna update.

“Brianna will make a full recovery. It appears that she drank too much vodka, but she is denying having drunk it. We think her drink may have been spiked, so we're going to do a full search of the rooms,” she informed us.

"Alcohol, at St Andrews?" I gave my best-shocked look.

"Yes Harper, do any of you girls know anything about this?"

We all shook our heads.

"If any alcohol is found then the culprit will be in big trouble," Miss Crombie announced. "Come on." She held the door open and beckoned us to move outside our room.

I gulped and gave a quick glance at my bedside drawer where I'd put my bottle of perfume. Only it wasn't perfume at all. Instead, it contained some of the vodka I'd taken from my parent's drinks cabinet. I'd purposely put it in my not-so-good perfume bottle, as I knew my mom and the other girls wouldn't ever borrow it. It would have been too risky to put it in my Chanel No.5 bottle. I told myself to relax, I'd disguised it so well that they'd never find it.

No alcohol was found in the school, so no doubt the boys' school were blamed. I had my suspicions that Harper was behind it, but I knew better than to confront her about this. I hoped that Elliot didn't get the blame, after all, he'd been seen hanging out with Brianna. Then again without proof, they couldn't pin anything on him so he'd be fine, wouldn't he? I hoped so.

The dance hadn't gone to plan. Worse still, it seemed unlikely that they'd be another one anytime soon. I blamed Brianna for it, even though I doubted she'd drunk vodka knowingly. Still, she should have known better than to go after Elliot, as that was always going to cause problems. A boy as cute and sweet as him needed to be with someone as pretty and popular as me.

She'd learned a lesson the hard way. *Girl World* had no room for pushovers or cry-babies. It was ruthless and hard at times. Only the strong survived and the weak, well, they threw up over the cute boy and got carted off in an ambulance.

Chapter Nine - The New Girl

I was expecting Brianna to return and drive us all mad with her whining. A week passed by and she still hadn't returned. The rest of us were enjoying the peace, it made us realize just how loud Brianna actually was. It was as peaceful as a spa retreat without her here.

When Syd, Taylor and I were called into Miss Braun's office, we knew that it was going to be about Brianna. Maybe she'd asked to move rooms? Perhaps she'd blamed us for what'd happened? Maybe aliens had abducted her? (here's hoping this had happened!)

Miss Braun sipped at her glass of water before she looked up at us all, and coughed to clear her voice.

"I'm afraid that Brianna's parents have decided it best to remove her from our school. Therefore, she won't be returning."

We all exchanged surprised looks with each other. We didn't think that she'd never return. Still, I found myself thinking about the extra storage space her bed would provide.

"I know this is a shock for you all, but I have some exciting news to brighten your spirits," Miss Braun announced.

We all looked at her with interest, wondering what the news was.

"As you may all know, every year we give away one charitable position which allows one girl free admittance. This time it's your year's turn. In light of recent happenings, we have a spare bed. Therefore, I've decided that the girl who's been given this excellent opportunity no longer has to wait until the start of the new academic year."

"A new girl." I couldn't hide my shock. "I hope she up to my high standards as you do realize my parents pay a fortune to have me educated here?"

"Harper, the alcohol culprit was never found," Miss Braun looked directly at me. "But sometimes I like to think that karma works well in the world."

Okay, so I didn't know what she meant by that.

"Miss, does this mean this girl will have Brianna's bed?" Sydney asked.

"Yes, Sydney, she will your new roommate."

"But we don't have the room for another girl. It's barbaric that four of us were expected to all squash in there," I protested.

"I'm sure you'll survive," Miss Braun remarked. "The new girl will be arriving this evening; I trust you will all make her feel welcome."

Sydney and Taylor nodded in agreement, so I reluctantly did the same. Brianna was annoying, but at least her parents had actually paid to send her here. It seemed so unfair that this new girl had just got in here for free.

Sydney

A new girl, already! Brianna's bed was barely cold. This was a bedroom big enough for one person, two at the most. Three people sharing it was bad enough, but four was ridiculous. Anyone would think this school was short of money. I wondered if Miss Braun had piles of notes in her office that she sniffed and counted each night?

I felt bad for Brianna, as I knew what it was like to move schools without having a chance to say goodbye to anyone. She may have been a hyperactive giggle machine, but she probably hadn't deserved this.

Study time arrived, but none of us were actually studying. Instead, we were discussing what the new girl would be like.

"She'd better not giggle like Brianna did, or I'm making her switch rooms with Tiff," Harper commented.

"She'd better keep to her side of the room and not steal my stuff," I said grumpily.

"She's getting in for free, so she's bound to be rough," Harper responded.

"We should lock away our valuables." Taylor gave a worried look.

"What valuables?" Harper snorted. "All your stuff sucks Taylor."

Taylor blushed, but she didn't say anything back.

I wasn't thrilled at the thought of having to share this already cramped space with another girl. Although, I had to admit that it would be good not to be the new girl anymore. I wondered how the new girl would fair with Harper's ridiculous initiation test. She definitely wouldn't do as well as I did.

There was a knock at the door, and we all exchanged curious looks. The door opened, and Miss Crombie peered her head around it.

"Hey girls." She smiled at us before she walked into the room.

A new girl stepped in behind her, she was a similar height and size to me, but that was where the similarities ended. She had messy chin-length brown hair and was wearing a tracksuit jacket and black pants with scuffs on them.

"Hi." she gave a sly smile. "I'm Lisa."

Book 3

Insane

Chapter One – The New Girl

I stared at the new girl, to say she was scruffy would have been a HUGE understatement. Her brown bob looked like she'd taken the kitchen scissors to it and her boots…shudder! Please, don't even get me started on those.

Miss Crombie was standing there with a smile on her face. She was lucky that I hadn't fainted from the shock. They couldn't seriously expect me to share a room with someone who actually chose to wear such shabby clothes. My parents were worth millions, and therefore I was too, I couldn't be forced to associate with the likes of her. This was worse than awful, this was barbaric.

I couldn't talk, I was in too much shock. It seemed that Sydney felt the same, as she wasn't saying anything either. We both stood there staring at the new girl, our arms folded and unimpressed looks on our faces. I knew that it wouldn't be long before Miss Crombie said something stupid and then forced us to be nice to her. I wanted to tell her where she could put her niceness and that I was entitled to be able to choose with whom I associated.

"Um, hi." Taylor broke the standoff. "I'm Taylor."

"Hey," Lisa muttered, as she stared down at her ugly boots.

This was worse than my nightmare about failing my exams or being naked in assembly. I didn't want to talk to this girl.

"These are my friends Harper and Sydney." Taylor gestured to us.

My expression didn't falter, although I did give the slightest of eye rolls when Taylor referred to me as her friend. Just because we shared a room and I ordered her about on occasion, didn't mean that we were friends.

"They are quiet at first when they meet new people," Taylor continued.

Jeez, could this be any more awkward?

"I'll leave you in the capable hands of these girls." Miss Crombie looked at Lisa. "I'm sure they will do their best to make you feel settled. If you have any questions, ask Harper as she's a veteran." She chuckled to herself.

A veteran, seriously? She made it sound like I'd never left this place. Lisa gave her a nod and then she left. There was an awkward silence as we all sussed each other out. Taylor opened her mouth to no doubt say something stupid, but Sydney beat her to it (thankfully.)

"Where are you from?" Sydney raised an eyebrow.

"Around," Lisa croaked.

"Is it that bad you can't even tell us?" Sydney stuck up her nose. She really could play the role of an upper-class snob extremely well.

Lisa continued to look at her boots and didn't reply. I smirked to myself. It seemed that Sydney had put the new girl in her place.
"You do realize that our parents pay $70,000 a year to send us here? We are all from fine and upstanding families. How have you managed to wrangle your way in for free?" Sydney asked.

Lisa didn't say anything, jeez, she was such a loser.

"She's a charity case. It doesn't matter where she has come from, by the looks of her; it's clearly a slum somewhere," I remarked with as much sarcasm as my voice could muster.

"Leave her alone," Taylor snapped.

My smirk grew larger. "Wow, Taylor, I thought you didn't have a backbone."

"Go away and hide, so I don't have to look at those disgusting boots." I shooed my hand at her.

"You don't need to be so mean," Taylor muttered.

"What was that?" I grinned at Taylor, daring her to say something else.

She didn't reply, it seemed that Taylor's fighting spirit had been short-lived.

"Yeah, I guess I'm a charity case," Lisa shrugged. "But I'm proud of where I come from and of my parents."

"What are their occupations?" Sydney asked.

"They are probably on unemployment benefits, living off the money that our parents pay in taxes," I snarked.

Lisa shook her head slowly. "Which bed is mine?"

Sydney and I both stared at her. This girl was obviously a massive loser.

"That one," Taylor pointed to the bed next to hers.

"Thanks," she smiled.

We all watched as she walked over to her bed and bounced down onto it.

"I doubt she's ever slept on a proper bed before," Sydney remarked.

"Yeah, she's probably used to some moldy old mattress on the floor," I snorted.

Taylor glared at me, but she didn't say anything. I stared back at her, and she instantly altered her gaze downwards. She knew that if I wanted to, I could make her life a misery.

I put my headphones in and blasted out music as I scrolled through my phone. I made the odd glance over at the new girl and watched as she unpacked her gross belongings. She didn't belong here and girls like her never would.

Chapter Two – Oh!

Naturally, everyone in the school was gossiping about the new girl. I even heard a couple of the teachers talking about her. I mean, seriously, she was just some charity case girl with terrible taste in fashion.

I couldn't escape the rumors, especially as the other girls thought that I knew everything about the new girl just because I was forced to share a room with her. I was walking back from breakfast by myself, so I could get some peace when Amy rushed up alongside me.
"Hi Syd." She smiled.
"Hi." I resisted the urge to roll my eyes. "And it's Sydney."

"I heard that both of the new girl's parents are in prison," she spluttered. "Is it true?"

"How would I know?"

"Well, she's your roommate."

"So?" I frowned. "I've known the girl for less than a day, so I hardly know her life story or anything."

"She must have told you something. Do you think that she grew up in prison with them? Do you think that she's dangerous?"

"I told you, I don't know," I quickened my pace. This was getting really irritating. I had better things to think about.

"I'm surprised you managed to sleep with her in your room." Amy matched her pace to keep up with me. "She could have smuggled a knife in or anything."

"I need to go to my room." I veered off around the corner.

"I'd sleep with one eye open if I were you," Amy called out.

"Bye Amy," I shouted, without turning back to look at her. I walked along the corridor towards my room; two of the girls from next door were talking outside their door. They fell silent when they saw me and looked at me like I was full of information. Here we go again, I said to myself.

"Is it true that the new girl was abandoned at birth?" Grace asked.

"No idea." I shrugged as I carried on walking.

"Wait!" Tiff shouted after me, and I reluctantly stopped walking and spun around. "It's pretty obvious that she was the girl from the woods. They found her there as a toddler. Bears raised her, so she had to be taught how to act like a human."

"That is ridiculous." I rolled my eyes. "Lisa's from a poor family, that's all. She wasn't abandoned and bought up by wild animals, instead, Miss Braun felt sorry for her, so she let her come here for free. End of the story!" I spun back around and walked up to my door.

"Well, I still think she's the girl from the woods," Tiff replied.

"Whatever," I said under my breath as I stepped into my room. Why couldn't they all shut up about the new girl? She was just some charity case nobody. She was only here because Brianna was too embarrassed to come back after the dance incident. Brianna was a hyped-up ball of energy, but at least her parents weren't poor.

I had the room to myself as the others were still at breakfast. I grabbed my books and hugged them as I sat on the edge of my bed and stared over at the new girl's bed. I pictured Brianna bouncing up and down on it and Miss Crombie marching in and giving her a detention. I remembered when she covered her bed in clothes options for the dance and threw a tantrum because she hated them all. I pictured her doing that stupid robot walk across the room in an attempt to learn how to talk to boys.

Brianna was majorly annoying, immature and naïve but she was also funny, kind and entertaining. I guess I missed her, and I resented the new girl for taking her place. Brianna had deserved to be here, but Lisa didn't. Still hugging my books,

I let out a sigh, then stood up. As I walked across the room, I took a second glance at Brianna's old bed that no longer had her over-loved cuddly bear on it. Change was inevitable. It was always going to happen. I could put up with change, but that didn't mean that I had to like it, especially when it seemed unjust.

I was stuck here, Brianna had gone, and the new girl fitting in at St Andrew's was about as likely as mom charging into my room and telling me she missed me.

I feigned interest in my sloppy porridge, so I didn't have to communicate with the new girl or the girls that had swarmed around her like flies to a dead bunny. I now totally understood why Sydney wolfed down her breakfast and then hurried off. She wasn't penned in by a bunch of tragic onlookers. Jeez, hadn't they ever seen a poor girl before?
"Do you like it here?" Emma asked her.

I rolled my eyes, trust that girl to come up with such an annoying question.

"Yeah, I guess." Lisa shrugged before she took a big bite out of her toast.

"Have you ever seen a school as big as this before?" Amy elbowed Taylor to the side so she could get closer to Lisa.

"Ow!" Taylor muttered.

"I guess not," she mumbled with her mouth full.

"Your hairstyle is cute. Where do you get it done?" Hannah asked.

"She's not going to go to a top salon, is she? I mean, she isn't rich," Amy commented.

"It doesn't mean her hairstyle isn't cute," Hannah said sounding flustered and giving Amy a dirty look.

"Lisa, what's your house like?" Grace asked.

"Grace, you can't ask that. She might not live in a house," Tiff hissed at her.

"Sorry," Grace muttered.

"I had a house," Lisa replied.

The stupid questions were winding me up. I resisted the urge to pour my gross porridge over them and storm off. It just seemed like far too much effort to have to navigate through the swarm of girls.

Taylor had finished her breakfast ages ago but was staring at the new girl like she was a puppy waiting to be taken for walkies. As soon as Lisa had put the last bit of toast into her mouth, Taylor grabbed her arm. "Are you ready for the tour now?" she asked.

"Sure." Lisa smiled.

"I'll come too," Amy said.

"Me too," Tiff added.

Soon the majority of girls were following the new girl and a bemused looking Taylor. Finally, I could finish my breakfast in peace. Taylor was acting like the new girl's best friend...so lame! I mean come on; she'd only known her for five minutes. It was tragic how desperate for a friend she was. I couldn't face any more porridge, it was disgusting. I sat there for a few seconds to compose myself before I stood up. That's when I noticed that Meg (one of the older girls) was walking over to me.

"Hi Harper, it's unusual to see you alone." Meg grinned.

"I didn't want to go on Taylor's boring school tour."

"Good point." She chuckled. "I heard that the new girl is so poor that she lives in a tent with a hole in it."

"That wouldn't surprise me given the state of her," I replied. "I better get to my lesson. I don't want the new girl getting poor germs on my seat."

"Bye Harper." Meg smirked at me.

"Bye."

Some things in life were black and white, and elegance and class were some of those things; you either had it or you didn't. I had it, and the new girl didn't, and there was nothing she could do to change this.

The first lesson of the day was Harper's favorite…not! It was cooking with Miss Ekelby. Okay, so it wasn't the most brain-inducing of subjects, but cooking was a novelty to me. Mom had been so strict with me on what I could eat…so making cakes and casseroles was rather fun.

Lisa arrived at class with a bunch of the other girls buzzing around her, including Taylor who seemed incapable of leaving her alone. I looked at Harper, who was sitting next to me and rolled my eyes. She laughed and then shook her head.

"I wonder what Taylor's parents would think of her new best friend?" she whispered to me.

I chuckled. I imagined taking Lisa back to meet my parents. My mom would have totally freaked out. It would have been hilarious.

"Morning girls." Miss Ekelby gave a wide smile. "I know you're all very excited about making pumpkin pie."

Harper snorted, but Miss Ekelby chose to ignore it.

"I know that I am. But first of all, I see that we have a new girl with us. I'm sure everyone here would love to learn a bit about you." She gestured her over.
Lisa exchanged a look with Taylor before she walked over to Miss Ekelby. I looked at Harper, and she smirked back, we both thought that this was going to be good.

"Hi, I'm Lisa," she croaked. "So, I'm an orphan."

This received gasps from most of the girls.

"My parents were double agents working in North Korea. They were really talented and brave, but this didn't stop them from being captured while they were trying to extract documents about the nuclear weapons programme. Initially, they were imprisoned in a prison camp deep in the freezing north. For two years they were starved and beaten. My mom's body gave up first, and she passed away. When she passed, my dad gave up hope. He refused to eat any more of the maggot infested soup they were given once a day. Two weeks later he joined by mom in heaven."

Everyone was sitting there shocked. It felt as though an invisible sheet of silence was covering us. Some of the girls were quietly sobbing to themselves, and I noticed that even Harper had tears in her eyes.

Miss Ekleby was trying desperately hard to keep composed, but this was clearly a struggle for her. "Th-thank you Lisa, Th-thank you for sharing," she sobbed.

Lisa walked back over to her workbench. A teary-eyed Taylor engulfed her in a hug. Miss Ekelby looked flustered, and the rest of the girls were messes. The only person who seemed to be holding it together was Lisa, so I guessed that what'd happened with her parents must have been a while ago. A million thoughts were flying around my head, but I didn't want to bombard her with them. She had been through so much, I felt terrible for the way that I'd treated her, but I hadn't realized what she'd gone through. My mom and dad were super annoying, but I couldn't imagine ever losing them.

I looked at Harper, and she was still glassy-eyed. I felt terrible about the way I'd treated Lisa, and I wondered if she did too? I couldn't change the way I'd treated Lisa, but I could make an effort to be nicer to her from now on. That could wait until later though, as right now, I had a pumpkin pie to make.

***

We were all sat at our usual table in the cafeteria. A few extra girls had squashed in at our table, all of them desperate to get close to Lisa. Harper and I hadn't said anything to her yet. I guessed she was waiting for the right moment like I was.

"Be right back," Lisa said to Taylor as she stood up. "I'm going to the bathroom."

"I'll come with you." Taylor jumped up to her feet. "I'll

show you the way."

"Thanks." Lisa grinned.

I couldn't help but roll my eyes, Taylor was such a suck-up.

Jesse, a tousle-haired girl from the year above us, wandered over. "Harper, when's the new girl's initiation starting?" she asked.

I stared at Harper, curious as to how she'd respond.

"It's not. Lisa's already passed," Harper replied.

Jesse gave Harper a confused look.

"But everyone new here has to do it," she replied.

"Not her, okay? Make sure that everyone is nice to her or they'll have me to answer to."

"Right, okay." Jesse continued to look puzzled. "I'll tell the others."

I gave a slight smile. It turned out that Harper did have a heart after all, and I was proud of her, not that I was going to tell her that.

A bemused Jesse walked off to her friends, and Lisa and Taylor returned. The other girls instantly bunched up to allow room for them. I rolled my eyes, the way the other girls were acting was so pathetic, they only liked Lisa because she was new and different.

Harper smiled at Lisa. "Don't worry. You can stick with me and then you'll settle right in here."

Lisa put down her fork and gave Harper a scrutinizing look which continued for several seconds. Everyone else at the table was deadly silent as they watched what was happening. "When I arrived, you ignored me and put me down. Now, you're acting like you're my best friend. I don't get that type of falseness, Harper."

Harper's mouth gaped wide open. "I-I didn't mean it. I d-didn't k-know," she spluttered.

Lisa leaned across the table and stared directly at Harper. "You're a snob and a nasty girl. Yes, your parents are rich, but that's no reason to treat people like they're beneath you," she said in a low and robust voice.

I gasped, I'm sure that nobody had EVER dared to speak to Harper like that before; nobody!

I joined the rest of the girls in looking on with shocked anticipation. This was better than the final of The Bachelor. I had no idea how Harper would react or if Lisa was in mortal danger.

Harper's face grew redder-and-redder, and I wasn't sure if it was from embarrassment or anger. "You had better pull your head in new girl. Yes, your parents may have died as heroes, but around here you're just plain old Lisa, the charity girl," she said assertively.

The two girls stared at each other, venom in their eyes. Neither one wanted to look away first. It was uncomfortable to watch, the silence was deafening, and I was starting to feel queasy. I tugged at my shirt collar and willed for someone to break the awkwardness soon.

Taylor stood up, pushed her chair and then tapped Lisa on the shoulder. "Come on Lisa, and I'll give you a proper tour of the library before our next class," she said.

Clearly, Taylor couldn't take the atmosphere anymore either. I was impressed that she'd been the one to break it, I mean, only someone completely stupid or crazy would interrupt these two owl wannabes in a stare-off.

Lisa turned and smiled at Taylor and in doing so broke eye-contact with Harper.

"Thanks, Taylor, that'd be great." Lisa stood up and followed Taylor.

Harper was gripping tightly onto her fork; she looked furious. I watched as she stabbed her fork into a potato with force. I discreetly shuffled further away from her and then continued to eat my lunch.

I had no idea how Harper was going to deal with this situation; all I knew was that I couldn't wait to find out.

Chapter Three - Conflict

I was furious. How dare she talk to me like that. She was a pathetic charity case who should crawl back into the gutter she came from; the rat! I'd been kind to her because I'm a good person and she'd reacted like that!!! She's just a horrible, ordinary person who didn't belong here.

Worse still, I had to watch on as the other girls flocked around Lisa like she was something special. She was NOT special. She was nothing!!! It was all because of her stupid sob story. Yeah, what'd happened to her parents was sad, but she wasn't the only one who had to deal with hard stuff. At least her parents had loved her and hadn't abandoned her in a boarding school at the age of five. And to think that I was actually going to let her off the initiation test; NO CHANCE!!! Everyone else had done it, so she could too.

I walked into my room to find her sitting on Brianna's bed like she owned the place. I walked straight past her without giving her a second glance. Worse still, Taylor was all over her like a scabby rash. She was all: Can I get you anything Lisa? Do you like it here Lisa? You're such a strong, amazing person Lisa. Bleurgh, she was pathetic. Even more annoying than the fact Taylor was a suck-up, was the fact that Sydney was being sweet to Lisa too.

"You can borrow my stuff if you want, just ask." Sydney smiled at her.

I choked on the smuggled in chocolate bar I was eating. Seriously, Sydney was offering to lend out her clothes? It was rare for her to let anyone near them, so the fact she'd offered to lend them to Lisa was crazy.

"Thanks, what have you got?" Lisa muttered. She certainly didn't sound very grateful.

Sydney rooted through her clothes drawer and pulled out a few items. "How about this?" A cute red blouse was in her hands. "Or this?" She held up a baby blue colored t-shirt.

"Thanks, but they wouldn't suit my style," she replied.

"Oh! Okay." Sydney tried to hide the hurt from her voice. "Ooh, I have a cute jacket that you would look great in."

"No offense or anything, but I wouldn't be seen dead in

your clothes."

There was an awkward silence. I looked at Sydney to gauge her reaction. She had turned as red as the blouse she'd offered to lend to Lisa. Her expensive, designer clothes were very important to her, so the way Lisa had reacted would have stung. The new girl really was a piece of work. I hated her, and I wanted her to go away, back to where she belonged.

Sydney looked like she was close to exploding and I wouldn't have blamed her if she had. Instead, she took a deep breath and forced a smile onto her face.

"No problem." Sydney shrugged before she walked into the bathroom and closed the door behind her.

I looked at Taylor, even she looked shocked. I didn't know if this was because Lisa had been so rude or because Sydney hadn't blasted at her. What was with the new girl? She had everyone under her spell and all because her parents had died as heroes.

A few minutes later Sydney returned, and she slumped down onto her bed with a book. Everyone was super quiet, and the atmosphere in here was awkward. So, it seemed the perfect time to drop the initiation shaped bomb on Lisa.

"Lisa, all new girls have to go through a set of initiation tests to prove their worth here. You don't get a free pass just because of your sob story." I stared at her.

Taylor looked like she wanted to say something but instead she bit her lip, a defeated look on her face.

"Whatever." Lisa shrugged.

"It's not easy, you know. You can't just stroll around the place and expect everyone else to help you. To pass you'll have to prove your worth. If you fail, you can get used to a life of no friends or privileges," I told her.

There was a brief silence as she absorbed my words, then she looked me directly in the eye. "Bring it on."

"Harper, you're being mean," Taylor eventually piped up. "Lisa shouldn't have to go through the initiation test."

"Lisa will do whatever I want her to," I yelled at Taylor. How dare she question my leadership. Such a brat!

Lisa stood up and walked over to me. I watched her with caution, wondering what she was going to do. She stopped in front of me and leaned over me so that I could feel her breath on my face. She had seriously crossed a line, this was my space, and she needed to get out of it.

"I can make my own decisions, but if this initiation test belongs to you, then I won't be bothering with it."

"The girls won't accept you, you'll be an outcast," I responded.

"Oh no." she smirked. "Face it, I - don't - want - to - join - your - group," she said extra slowly.

Sydney burst out laughing, and I shot her a stern look. Thanks a lot, Syd, really helpful!

"Whatever, your breath stinks like a sewer," I snapped. I could feel my heart rate rising rapidly and my hands were starting to shake with anger.

"Like I care." Lisa purposely breathed on me.

Great, now I had charity girl germs all over me. This girl was vile, and I couldn't take it anymore. I reached over, grabbed my pillow and started whacking her with it. She grabbed the pillow off her bed and started hitting me back with it. This wasn't a playful, girly pillow fight like they have in the movies; this was full force and brutal.

"I hate you!" she whacked me in the face.

"I hate you more!" I hit her in the side so that she wobbled on her feet.

"You're nothing but a horrible stuck-up cow."

"And you're nothing but a tragic charity case," I yelled.

I whacked her with my pillow again-and-again, and she whacked me back. Her hits hurt but I was too fueled by adrenaline and anger to register this fully, it was as though only me and this vile girl existed, and I badly wanted her to disappear.

"Ahem!" a voice said assertively.

I followed the sound of the voice and stopped still, my pillow still mid-air when I saw that Miss Crombie was watching us. I don't know if Lisa hadn't heard Miss Crombie or if she just didn't care, either way, she whacked me in the side with her pillow. I instinctively hit her back and chose to disregard Miss Crombie's pleas for us to stop.

Firm hands held us apart. I gripped onto my pillow and looked past Miss Crombie and straight at Lisa. She dropped her pillow down by her side and shook her head at me.

"What on earth has caused this disgraceful behavior?" She glared at us.

I was about to tell her that it was all Lisa's fault and had nothing to do with me, but Lisa managed to get her words out first.

"It was my fault," she announced.

I breathed a sigh of relief. The last thing I wanted was a month's worth of detentions for daring to have a pillow fight with the new girl. It wasn't even my fault. She had started it.

"I suppose I was mean because Sydney was trying to make me wear her clothes and I didn't want to. Then Harper was trying to make me do her initiation test, and I didn't want to do that either," she sniffed.

My face dropped; the new girl knew exactly what she was doing. The staff was never meant to find out about the initiation test. Lisa had just snitched.

"Harper, Sydney, Taylor, go to Miss Braun's office, now!" Miss Crombie said as she gave us an extra sour look.

I mumbled some words of protest under my breath before I begrudgingly trudged across the room. As I passed Lisa, I noticed the slight smirk on her ugly face.

"Miss, this isn't far," Sydney moaned. "I was being nice to the new girl."

Miss Crombie ignored her. She signaled with her hands so that we quickened up our pace. I imagined Lisa sitting alone in my room, an undeserved smug look on her stupid face. I hated her, really hated her. This was my school, not hers. She was a charity case nobody, and she needed to know her place. How dare she snitch on me and refuse to do my initiation test. She couldn't expect to just stroll in here, and for it to be all cupcakes and sparkle. There was a hierarchy, and I was at the top, and she was at the bottom.

Nobody snitched on me and got away with it. NOBODY!

Chapter Four – The Inquisition

Standing outside of Miss Braun's office was not how I wanted to spend my free time. This was totally unfair; I had only been nice to Lisa. I hadn't hit her with my pillow, so why was I in line to be questioned? This majorly sucked!

Miss Crombie stepped out of Miss Braun's office and called Harper into it. So, they had opted for the interview us one-at-a-time technique, this was totally lame and meant that I was going to be stuck here even longer. As Harper passed me, she shot me a *don't land me in it* look. I just smiled at her. I wasn't sure if I was going to tell on her or keep quiet. I'd see how the moment took me, when I got in there.

Miss Crombie shot Taylor and me a dirty look before she walked off. I bet she fed off all this drama, as it was the only excitement in her otherwise dull life.

Time ticked by slowly. Taylor remained mouse-like quiet, so I didn't even bother trying to communicate with her. Instead, I filled my time by taking in my mundane surroundings. There was a stain on the duck-egg colored wall, the picture adjacent to me hung slightly wonky, and there was an unpleasant bleach smell.

Boring…Boring…Boring. I sang a song in my head and willed for Harper to hurry up. No doubt she was putting on the waterworks and protesting her innocence. I rolled my eyes and gave a shake of my head. 'Hurry up, hurry up, hurry up,' I chanted in my head.

I slumped further down in the hard chair. It wasn't fair that the new girl wasn't sitting here instead of me. I was an innocent bystander. I couldn't have been expected to have separated a pillow-fight between Harper and Lisa! I could have lost a nail or worse. Besides, none of this was my fault. I'd been kind to Lisa. I'd even offered to lend her some of my clothes. I'd been trying to do her a favor, as let's face it, her clothing is dreadful. Instead of being grateful she'd been rude, which was totally uncalled for. I didn't blame Harper for changing her mind about Lisa doing the initiation tasks, and I also got why she started the pillow fight. Lisa wasn't a nice person, and she was clueless and inconsiderate when it came to sharing a room.

Finally, the door to Miss Braun's office opened, and Harper followed the headmistress out and sat down in the empty seat next to Taylor.
"No talking," she glared at them before her eyes stopped on me. "Sydney." She beckoned me forward.

I followed Miss Braun into her office and sunk into the low chair in front of her desk. She closed the door and then strolled across the room and took her seat. She looked at me, sighed and then looked down at the scribbled notes in front of her. I tried to discreetly look over, so I could read them, but they were too far away. They must have been the notes she'd written when she'd questioned Harper. I was desperate to learn what they said, as this would have been a lot easier if I'd known how Harper had spun it.

Miss Braun turned onto a fresh page and then picked up her gold pen. "So, Sydney, did you offer Lisa the use of some of your clothes?" She stared at me.
I didn't understand why this was even a question. Was being nice a crime? Jeez, this was ridiculous.

"Yes, I did, I noticed that she doesn't own many clothes and I thought that it would be a nice gesture to let her borrow some of mine. I know how hard it is being new here, so I thought that it was a nice thing to do and would make her feel more included."

"That was a lovely thing to do," she commented. "Am I right in believing that she didn't accept your kind offer?"

"She didn't."

"Did you feel offended by this?" Miss Braun asked.

"Not at all." I smiled.

"Harper seems to think differently." She turned the page back on her notes and glanced down at them. "Apparently, you vanished into the bathroom and were gone for quite some time."

I just needed to go to the toilet." I laughed.

"Were you made to partake in an initiation test?" she asked.

I paused for thought, as I knew that I needed to answer this carefully. Not only could my answer land Harper in heaps of trouble but I could have caused problems for myself too. I had broken a bunch of rules during my initiation test, and I knew that Miss Braun wouldn't have been impressed by this.

"Yes," I eventually replied. "But it was nothing, just some harmless challenges."

"Such as?" she raised an eyebrow. She was like a bloodhound on the scent of a wounded animal.

I racked my brain trying to think up the least naughty ones. "Well, I had to be Harper's slave for a week."

"What!" she gave a horrified look. "What do you mean a slave?"

"I had to collect Harper's food for her and serve her at her table." I shrugged. "It was silly stuff really, no big deal."

"And the other initiation tests, what were they?"

I didn't want to tell her anymore. I knew I had to keep my cool and act like they were nothing of importance.

"Um," I gave her my best thinking look. "I can't remember in detail."

"What did they involve?" she asked.

"Um, well, there was a privacy test," I replied.

"Which was?"

"I don't recall the details," I lied.

"Sydney, I don't believe for a second that a girl as smart as you can't remember the initiation tests she was made to do."

"Well, it was silly stuff really. My roommates went through my clothes and wore some of them, but it didn't matter, they're only clothes." I definitely wasn't going to tell her how they barged in on me in the bathroom and refused to let me get changed in peace.

"Okay, what were the other parts of this test?" Miss Braun asked.

I couldn't tell her about sneaking out of the school grounds or how I was locked out of my corridor all night and was found by the janitor sleeping in a cardboard box.

"They tested me on my ability to accept that people gossip. They gossiped about my house burning down and blamed me for it. They also teased me about my burns." I rubbed the red marks on my arm. I made my eyes tear up (a skill I'd learned to perfect) for added effect. There was no way that I was getting into trouble for this. If Harper and Taylor did, then that wasn't my problem, they could blame Lisa for it, seeing as she'd snitched to Miss Crombie about the initiation.

She was silent as she absorbed my words, then she stood up and walked around her desk. I didn't know what she was going to say or do, so when she leaned over and patted me on the shoulder, I had to clamp my teeth down on my gums to stop myself from laughing out in shock.

"Girls can be so very mean." She sighed. "Thank you, Sydney. You can wait outside while I talk to Taylor."

I gave her a nod and then followed her across the office. She held the door open and let me pass and then her eyes fixed on a coy looking Taylor. I purposely looked away from Harper and stared at the mark on the wall.

"What did you say?" Harper hissed as me.

I just shrugged and gave her a slight smile. She didn't say anything else, although I could tell from the concerned look in her eyes that she wanted to say more. She probably didn't want to chance Miss Braun hearing us, after all, we were meant to be sitting here in silence. It didn't matter anyway, and it's not like I could change what I'd said to Miss Braun. This was all Lisa's fault anyway, not mine.

Ten minutes later Miss Braun called us back into her office. We both sat down either side of a teary-eyed Taylor. I saw Harper give her a 'what have you said?' stare. Harper was clearly a girl on the edge, I guess it sucked to be her right now.

It felt as though Miss Braun was purposely keeping us in suspense. She reread her notes and scratched at her nose before she finally looked at us. "Initiation tests are unkind, silly and most of all they are dangerous. I will not have them happening in my school, do I make myself clear?" She looked at Harper.

Harper gave a weak nod. She knew better than to cross an angry Miss Braun, but I knew that Harper would be super annoyed with what had happened.

"Starting a new school is a daunting enough experience without being coerced into silly challenges. All new students should be made to feel welcome and included, not isolated and bullied. This is not the St Andrew's way, and it is not acceptable."

"It wasn't bullying," Harper muttered.

"Is that right?" Miss Braun gave her a scrutinizing look. "Then what do you suppose bullying is?"

"It was just a few harmless tasks, that's all. It made them feel included and helped them get acquainted with the way of the school," Harper explained.

"Don't you think that talking to them in a friendly manner and offering to show them around the school would have been a better way of acquainting them with the school ways?"

Harper gave a reluctant nod.

"You didn't do this Harper; instead you made them feel isolated. That is bullying, and it is not acceptable behavior in my school." Miss Braun looked super angry, the frown lines on her forehead were the most prominent I'd ever seen them. I didn't want to be in her office anymore watching Harper and Taylor squirm; it was making me feel uncomfortable.

"Sydney, thank you for being honest with me." She smiled at me. "You can leave."

"Thanks, Miss Braun." I stood up and quick-walked out of the room.

I could feel Harper's eyes boring into me. Okay, so she was going to be mad because I told Miss Braun about some of the initiation tests, but this wasn't my fault, it was Lisa's. I would not be blamed for this. Besides, Harper knew the risks when she'd started the initiation tests. She'd just have to suck it up and take whatever punishment came her way. Then she could have it out with Lisa later.

Chapter Five – Academy Award Time

Miss Braun looked as angry as a dragon before it went in for its first strike. I was in trouble. Serious trouble!!! Thanks a lot, Sydney. She was meant to be my friend, but she'd ratted me out. Taylor was silently sobbing next to me, jeez, that girl was so pathetic. She'd probably caved in too and told Miss Braun all about the initiation tests. Why was I stuck in this school with a bunch of losers?

"Taylor." Miss Braun's gaze fixed on her. "You lied to me, and that is not acceptable."

"I'm s-sorry," she sniveled. Tears were running down her face and she looked hot and flushed.

Okay, so Taylor didn't rat me out. This didn't change the fact that she was still a loser, she was just a less weasel-like one.

"You will have detention every afternoon for the next week and will not be permitted to partake in any after-school activities for this period."

This made Taylor sob even harder. To be fair, it was a pretty harsh punishment for not being a snitch.

"W-what about the choir try-outs?" Taylor asked.

"I may make an exception for those, seeing as the choir is in desperate need of some enthusiastic members. My generosity ends there, and there will be no more exceptions for any other after-school activities."

"Thank you, Miss Braun, I appreciate your kindness." Taylor continued to sob.
Jeez, who cared about the stupid choir.

"Harper," Miss Braun looked at me, and I gulped. "I am disappointed in your mean and cruel behavior towards new students at this school. I honestly believed that you had more moral character and heart. I can't believe you would be so cruel. How dare you think that you are in charge of this school, you are a mere child who has no power over anything. It isn't up to you to decide who is accepted and who isn't."

"But Miss-"

"I don't want to hear your excuses. You can't wriggle your way out of this one. You're in a lot of trouble Harper. You will have two weeks' worth of detentions, be banned from all after-school activities for this period and your parents will be notified of your behavior."

I stared at her open-mouthed. There were so many thoughts racing around my head, but I couldn't find the right words to say.

"Taylor, you can leave." She gave her a brief disgusted look.

Taylor sobbed her way out of the room; pathetic.

"Harper." Her eyes fixed on me. "From now on I strongly suggest that you treat all students like you'd want to be treated yourself. If you ever pull a stunt like this again, then you will be expelled!"

Expelled...was she serious? I was the best thing about this school; without me it would be horrendous. How dare she talk to me the way she had and threaten me with expulsion. I wasn't that bothered about the detentions. I also didn't care about the activities ban as they were all boring anyway. But I definitely wasn't looking forward to my parents being notified. My mother had already threatened to leave me here for the summer if I misbehaved again. She wouldn't follow through with her threat, would she?

"I want you to write down everything about these initiation tests." Miss Braun placed a pen and a piece of paper down in front of me.

I picked up the pen and stared down at the blank page. I didn't know what to write because I didn't know which parts Sydney had told her. I needed time to talk to Sydney first or I could risk landing myself in even more trouble.

Think. Think. Think...

I could say I needed the bathroom, but Miss Braun would probably have escorted me there. I could pretend that I was feeling sick, but she wasn't dumb enough to fall for that. She was sitting there watching me like a bird of prey as she tapped her gold pen against her desk. Suddenly, a great idea popped into my head. I started it off with a couple of sniffs and then I began to sob. My crying grew more intense (I'm a pro) and then I pretended to struggle to breathe. I clutched my throat and gave frantic looks. Miss Braun ignored my academy performance, so I stepped it up a notch. I swayed from side-to-side before I pretended to faint by falling off my chair, landing on the floor with a thud!
I hit my head…ouch! But it got Miss Braun off her feet, so my genius plan had worked. As she hovered over me, I kept my eyes closed tight and didn't move. Miss Braun shouted out for help. This was followed by several minutes of havoc. I continued to pretend to be unconscious and I heard concerned voices talk around me.

"That bump on her head is growing bigger!"

"The paramedics are on their way."

"Don't move her in case her neck is broken."

Paramedics! How ridiculous. It was hard not to burst out laughing but because I was such a great actress I managed not to. The only downside was the fact that my head did actually hurt. I'd had to make the fall look real and to do that I'd basically had to fling myself off my chair. Yeah, bashing my head hadn't been planned but at least it looked convincing.

The paramedics arrived, and I pretended to come around as they fitted me with a neck brace.

"W-what h-happened?" I asked groggily.

"Harper, you fainted. We're going to take you to the hospital to run some tests," a cute, youngish paramedic said.

I was about to nod in response then remembered that I was in a neck brace and I was meant to be injured. So instead, I just let out a fresh round of tears.
There were no girls about as I was carried on a stretcher out to the ambulance. I imagined them all peering out of their bedrooms windows and gossiping about me. Miss Braun came to the hospital with me which was super embarrassing. I didn't want anyone there thinking that she was my grandma…shudder!

I was made to wear a hideous white gown and had x-rays and scans carried out on me. What a bore, but it beat being stuck in Miss Braun's stuffy office.

I was in a white room, and a doctor told me that all the tests had come back fine, then she started asking me questions. Lightbulb moment, I couldn't be punished for the initiation tests if I couldn't remember them.

"What's your full name?" the doctor asked.

"Ahh, someone called me Harper before," I muttered.

"You don't remember your surname?"

"I-I, no," I feigned concern.

"Do you know what date it is?"

"No," I replied.

"Where do you go to school?"

"Um, not sure. I think it's close by."

"Where do your parents live?"

The real answer was they were in Boston living in a mansion. I wanted so badly to be living there with them, but they acted like I didn't exist. I wasn't going to say this to the doctor though, as I needed to maintain my act.

"Do I have parents?"

She sighed and wrote something down on her notepad.

"Is there something wrong with me? Am I broken?" I gave her my best glassy-eyed look.

"There's no need for alarm," the doctor gave a faint smile. "You need to rest. We'll carry out a CT scan to be sure."

I forced myself to cry even more. "I just want to go home, but I don't know where that is."

The doctor gave me another slight smile and a reassuring pat on the shoulder before she walked off to talk to Miss Braun. When they'd finished talking the doctor walked out of the room, and a concerned looking Miss Braun walked over to me. This was going to be fun.

"How are you feeling Harper?" she looked at me with concern.

"Are you my grandmother?" I asked.

"No Harper, I'm not." She grimaced.
"Are you my great-grandmother?"

Okay, so that one may have been slightly over-the-top and resulted in her giving me a suspicious look.

"I'm Miss Braun, your school principal. Don't you remember me?"

"Oh, yeah. No, not really. Are you a nice or nasty principal?"

Yeah, I know, but I couldn't resist asking her that. This was way too much fun.
She ignored my question. "Your parents are flying over from Boston. They will be here in a few hours."

"That's nice," I replied before I closed my eyes and pretended to fall asleep.

I heard Miss Braun quietly walk off. It was obvious that she didn't care about me, she just didn't want to be sued. The long day caught up with me and soon I found myself drifting off, this time into a *real* sleep.

Chapter Six – My Parents

When I woke up, I was being wheeled along the stark white corridors. I watched the walls of whiteness blur past me. Scans, tests…blah, blah, blah! They were boring, but they beat being in school and getting into trouble.

After the CT scan, I was wheeled back to my room, where my frantic looking parents were waiting. They stood either side of my bed, and each gripped one of my hands.

"Darling, we've been so worried." My mom was looking at me with tear-stained cheeks. Had she been crying? My mom never cried. I actually felt a bit bad. Maybe they did care about me after all; at least a little bit. Still, that hasn't stopped them from abandoning me, so they deserved to feel some guilt.

"Hi, who are you?" I gave her a puzzled look.

She burst into tears and dad let go of my hand so that he could walk around to her and engulf her in a hug.

"We're your mom and dad, Harper, don't you remember us?" He looked at me.

I creased my forehead as I pretended to think. I even chewed on my nails for added effect, which was something I never normally did…gross! I let the silence build for a couple of minutes.

"I think I have a mom and dad, but I don't remember much about them," I whispered. "They left me all alone in a terrible place when I was just a little kid. I remember being so afraid as I cried myself to sleep every night but still, they never came back for me."

Both of them gasped and then a cascade of tears escaped from mom's eyes. Dad went as pale as his crisp white shirt, and for a moment I thought he was going to pass out. He let go of mom so that he could sit down in the chair next to my bed.

I was quite curious about what they'd say next, but then the doctor walked in with a clipboard in hand.
My parents flocked around her and bombarded her with questions about me and gave her pleading looks. They'd

never cared about me before, so why were they acting like they did now? Maybe it was just for show, as they didn't want to appear heartless.

"Harper has a mild concussion, but the tests show that there is no damage to her brain." She smiled.

My dad was a leading heart surgeon, so when he pulled her to the side, I knew it would be to quiz her further. My dad gave a few nods then when he was satisfied with what he'd been told he walked over to my still hysterical mom, placed his arm around her shoulders and gripped onto my hand.

"Darling, you're having trouble with your memory as it's your brain's way of resting for a while to get over the shock of the fall. But you're going to be okay Harper, and your memories will come back soon." Dad took a deep breath. "Right, I better get right back to Boston as I am operating tomorrow." He let go of my hand.

I felt my heart fall. I knew I didn't really have memory loss, but my father didn't know that, and he was willing to leave me here alone and go back to Boston. I was his daughter, why didn't he care? Real tears trickled down my cheeks, and the bump on the side of my head seemed to throb more.

"But daddy, I want you to stay," I wept.

My mom's eyes widened, "Harper, are you remembering us now? You must be, I don't see why you'd be so upset if you still saw us as strangers?"

Oops, so that was a slip-up.

I looked from mom to dad and rubbed the bump on my

head. "I think I have some memories of you, back before you put me in that place. They're fuzzy though, you know, like an out-of-focus picture."

Inside, I was smiling, but on the outside, I maintained my dazed expression. My parents looked shocked by my comment, touché! Take that, bad parents.
Dad looked torn, maybe a part of him did want to stay. I knew that his job was important, I just wanted him to put me first just this once.

"I'm sorry darling, but I do have to get back to Boston." He sighed.

"It's okay daddy, you must have a vital job," I said, careful not to trip up again.

"I do." he managed a faint smile. "I'm a surgeon, Harper. I fix people's hearts and if I'm not there, well, then it's possible that they could die."

This made me feel a bit guilty. Even though I needed my dad badly, it seemed that other people needed him more.

"Oh wow, I'm so proud of you," I whispered softly. "You should do whatever is most important to you. I'm sure mom will stay and look after me." I smiled up at her.

Mom frowned, obviously looking after her injured daughter wasn't as important as whatever business deal she currently had going on. Money was everything to her; unfortunately!

"I'll see you soon Harper." Dad leaned over me and kissed me on the forehead. "The summer holidays are just around the corner, and we can catch up then." He smiled at me, gave me a wave and then hurried across the room.

He hadn't even said goodbye to my mom, not that she seemed bothered, as she was too busy texting on her phone. I wanted her to talk to me. I even would have settled for her to have at least looked at me. Instead, she remained fixed to her phone. She'd been crying a few minutes ago, but now she was acting like she didn't care at all.

I closed my eyes and eventually sleep claimed me. When I woke up, my mom had gone. I was in a white gown, on a white bed in a white room, and I felt more alone than ever.

It was nice having some peace and not having to share my room with three other girls. Still, I found myself longing for my mom's company. I kept one eye fixed to the door, willing for her to walk in with my favorite chocolates.

I waited. And waited...and waited. But that night she never returned.

The next morning, she turned up in a perfectly ironed navy skirted suit and lipstick matching the berry red sunglasses that rested on the top of her head. I immediately stopped eating my breakfast and smiled at her.

"Morning mom."

"Morning, darling, how are you feeling this morning?" She sat down next to me and pulled out her phone.

"A bit better mom, but my memory is still fuzzy." I rubbed my head.

"That's nice darling," she muttered, as she typed out a text message. "The doctor says that your memory is mostly back now."

When the doctor had visited me earlier, I'd told her that most of my memories had returned, it was just the last few weeks that seemed hazy. How could Miss Braun possibly punish me for Sydney's initiation when I couldn't remember it?

"The doctor says you can go home now?" she quickly glanced up from her phone and smiled, before she looked back down at it.

Excitement took over me; this meant that I got to spend some quality time with my mom. She only ever stayed in the best hotels, and I didn't mind staying in one with her, we could drink mocktails by the pool and then take a stroll along the beach. Maybe, later on, we could go shopping in the best designer outlets, and I could get some new clothes that would make Sydney totally jealous. Then we could get our hair cut in a top hair salon, then finish off the day by going for dinner in the exquisite Italian restaurant that overlooked the beach.

"Come on honey; I've got enough time to drop you off back at school before I have to whizz off to catch my flight," she said.

My heart fell. Silent tears streamed out of my eyes and ran down my cheeks. I felt crushed, useless, unwanted. All I longed for was a day, just one measly day with her and she couldn't even give me that. I wiped my cheeks and then swung my legs over the side of the bed. Mom was too busy on her phone to notice that I was crying. Work, work, work, that was all she cared about. She certainly didn't care about me!

There was no way that I was begging her to stay; no way!!! I was not going to give her the satisfaction of knowing that I wanted her to stay and spend some time with me. I loved her. I just wished that she loved me.

Chapter Seven - Rumors

There were some serious rumors going around about Harper. I'd heard girls saying that she was in a coma. That Miss Braun had pushed her off her chair and given her concussion. That she'd been expelled. I'd even heard a rumor that she'd fallen out of the upstairs window and was going to spend the rest of her life in hospital. I didn't take much notice of the gossip, but I was curious as to where Harper was.

I guessed that wherever she was, she would be mad at me. After all, Miss Braun had landed me in it. She had basically told Harper that it was me who had ratted her out. I knew that Harper would be annoyed, but she had to understand that Miss Braun was super persistent. It was never my intention to get Harper into trouble. I just had to protect myself first. Harper was the same; I knew that she would have put herself first too.

It was lunchtime, and I'd popped back to my room to relax, as I knew that Taylor and Lisa were trying out for the school choir. I was laid out on my bed with my designer headphones in, and I was bobbing my head in time to the music. Suddenly the door swung open, and a glum-looking Harper rushed across the room, got into bed and buried herself beneath her bedcover.

I carried on listening to music. So, Harper hadn't been expelled, nor was she in a coma, and she clearly hadn't fallen out of a window. She did have a lump on her head, so maybe there was truth to the 'Miss Braun pushing her off her chair' rumor. Nah, I thought, as I shook my head. There's no way Miss Braun would have done that; however annoying Harper could be at times. There was a brief silence in between songs, in that time I could hear a faint sobbing sound. I took my headphones off and looked over at Harper. Her bedcover was shaking, and the sobs grew louder.

I walked over to her bed and knelt beside it. "Harper," I spoke gently. "Harper, are you okay?"

There was no response, so I just knelt there for a few minutes and didn't say anything. Harper rarely showed her vulnerable side. She was like me; she liked the world to think that she was strong and unbreakable. I knew that whatever had upset her was a big deal to her. Otherwise, she would have buried it away in the back of her mind.

"Harper, what's up?" I gently shook her.

She abruptly pulled the cover off herself and glared at me

through rubbed, sore eyes.

"What did you tell Miss Braun about the initiation tests?" she said aggressively.

"Only the parts about being your slave, having gossip spread about me and how you went through my clothes and wore them," I replied.

"I guess that's not so bad." She sighed.

"I didn't want to get either of us into trouble, but thanks to Lisa, Miss Braun knew about the initiation tests, so I had to tell her something."

"Make sure you stick to your story and don't say any more." Harper looked at me sternly.

"I won't." I smiled at her. "Seriously though Harper, what's wrong?"

She looked away from me.

"Come on. I'm your friend. You know that you can talk to me, right?"

The tears began to stream down her face. I hurried into the bathroom and got her some tissues. "Here," I said, as I passed them to her.

She took the tissues and blew her nose. "Thanks," she said in-between sobs.

"Okay, it's time to spill the beans. What's the matter?"

"My parents don't love me," she sobbed. "They don't care

about me at all. I thought that maybe they did deep down, but now I know that they don't. They couldn't wait to get away from me and go back to work. I'm just a nuisance to them, one that can be put away with money and forgotten about."

I felt sorry for the girl, mainly because I could relate to her. I knew what it felt like to always be put behind money and success. I thought my parents were mean and uncaring, but I was starting to think that maybe Harper's were even worse than mine.

"I'm sorry Harper," I rubbed her arm. "Parents really do suck, don't they?"

"Yes, they do." Harper half laughed in between sobs.

I gave a slight laugh back. "They should all be abandoned on an island without their phones or any luxuries," I said.

"Yeah." she laughed. "My parents would hate that."

"Mine too. It'd be funny to watch though," I smirked. "It could be called *Useless Parents Island*."

Harper gave a faint smile and then wiped the tears from her cheeks. "Don't you wish they would change, even if it was just for a day?"

"Yeah." I looked downwards. "I plan all the adventures we could go on in my head. It doesn't alter anything though as they'll never change," I sighed.

"Yeah, mine won't either." Harper sighed. For a moment, we were both lost in our thoughts.

The door burst open, and Taylor sang her way into the room. I grinned at Harper as I placed my hands over my ears.

"Harper, you're back." Taylor walked over and stood next to me. "How're you feeling?"

"I'm good, I just have a headache." Harper looked at me and rolled her eyes.

"Thank you for not spilling the beans about the initiation tests to Miss Braun."

"That's okay." Taylor shrugged. "So, um, what was your punishment?"

"I'm not sure, I conveniently fainted and lost my memory when I was meant to be telling Miss Braun all about it." Harper smirked and winked at us.

"You sneaky little devil," I laughed. Harper was really very clever.

Harper and Taylor both started to laugh too. The door opened, and Lisa strolled into the room.

"What's so funny?" Lisa asked. "Oh, you're back." She looked at Harper.

"Yes, I'm back. And it's none of your business you little gutter rat," Harper snarled at her.

Taylor and I exchanged shocked looks.

"Whatever," Lisa hissed back before she walked into the bathroom and slammed the door shut.

One thing was for sure, Harper and Lisa were two girls that were never going to get along!

Harper

My fake faint and fall planned had worked perfectly. Taylor spent the rest of the week going to her detentions, but Miss Braun never bought my punishment up with me again. I was off the hook, and it was all because I was a genius.

Naturally, everyone was talking about me. Sydney told me about some of the rumors that had been spread about me – falling out of a window, seriously? Of course, I'd been the hot gossip, I was the original wild child, and this was my school, regardless of what snotty-nosed Miss Braun said. I was untouchable, and that decrepit old principal knew it.

This was all the new girl's fault anyway. She was a gutter rat snitch, and I hated her. If she'd come here knowing her place, then it would have been easier to put up with her. She should have been grateful. She was coming here for free. Instead, she was vile and nasty. I wanted her out of my room, out of my school, out of my life. How though? As much as I hated to admit it, the girl was pretty smart, and she'd also won over most of the dull-headed girls in our class.

Wherever she went the likes of Taylor and Amy were usually chasing after her. I caught Taylor carrying Lisa's tray over to her, that annoyed me, Lisa should have been my servant during her initiation, not making the other kids serve her.

Yes, she had a sob story, but that shouldn't have given her free access into my school. Miss Braun needed to up her vetting process as this was ridiculous. A girl like Lisa made the place look scruffy, how could Miss Braun be accepting of that? It seemed evident that no one else was going to do anything about Lisa so as usual, it was down to me to sort the problem out. As I thought about this my mouth curled into a smirk, after-all, she was nothing more than a nobody, a loser, a charity.

At lunchtime and I was sitting at my usual spot surrounded by the usual crowd. This was how it was meant to be as I was in charge around here.

"Was it scary being in the hospital alone?" Amy leaned over her tray and beamed at me.

"No Amy." I gave a definitive shake of my head. "I don't get scared."

"But people die in there, and their ghosts haunt the corridors."

I laughed so hard I spluttered out some of my water and specks landed on Sydney's arm (which she immediately wiped off) and Amy's blouse (she didn't even try rubbing it off.) Taylor and some of the other girls laughed at this.

Lisa walked over carrying her tray and scrunched up her nose as she looked at us. Taylor instantly stopped laughing and made the other girls move up to make room for her. She even let her have her chair and hurried off to get one from another table for herself. I grimaced at this. They should have made her stand there, like the loser she was. I ate my lunch and brewed in silence. Everything about the girl annoyed me, her she-thought-she-was-something-special look, the way her nose was too big for her ugly face and her stupid botched-up hairstyle.

Lisa got up to go and refill her glass. I was surprised she wasn't making Taylor or one of the other girls do it because she was so lazy.

"Hey Charity, get me one too." I held out my empty glass.

Most of the girls fell silent, and a few of them gasped. Then the giggles started, faint but enough to prompt me to carry on. "The water is free here. Hold on, everything is free for you!"

There were more shocked gasps from the other girls. Lisa snatched my glass from me and walked over to the water dispenser. I sat there smiling to myself. I'd put her in her place.

"Charity, is that your new name for her now?" Sydney asked, raising an eyebrow.

"That's her name, full stop." I smirked.

Sydney rolled her eyes, gave a brief laugh and then stuck a forkful of pasta into her mouth.

Taylor was giving me her usual *I want to say something, but I can't because I am a sniveling mouse* look.

"Yes?" I looked at Taylor, daring her to say something.

"Nothing." Taylor looked down at her food and shifted uncomfortably in her seat.

That's right, I was in charge around here, and Taylor knew it would be easier for her not to cross me. She knew her place at this school, and it was way below me.

Charity case was walking over to me with a smile on her face. "Here you go Harper." She lifted both glasses and poured them over me before I had time to react.

The water drenched my hair and caused strands to stick to my face. My blouse had gone see-through and felt like it had been glued to my skin. I looked down with horror. My white bra was now visible to everyone. I gasped and immediately covered my chest with my arms.

That's when I realized that most of the other girls were laughing; they were laughing at me! How dare they! I stood up, pushing my chair back so forcefully that it clattered to the ground. Lisa was stood there, a proud grin on her face. My anger bubbled over, and before I could even register what I was doing, I leaped across the table and knocked her to the ground.

I heard squeals from the other girls, but I didn't care. My focus was on the charity case and how much I despised her.

I sat on top of her and started pulling at her unkempt hair.

"You are nothing but a charity case. You don't belong here. I HATE you!!!" I yelled at her.

She grabbed my waist and shoved me off her. I fell with a thud onto the floor and before I had time to even sit up, she had jumped on top of me, pinned down my right arm and then slapped me across my face.

I screamed at her and hit her in the ribs with my free arm. She hit me back, which fuelled my anger and caused me to break free of her grasp and roll her over, so I was on top of her. We continued to roll around hitting and pulling on each other.

"Fight! Fight! Fight!" was chanted in the background.

The chanting didn't matter, and the other girls didn't matter. All that mattered was how much I wanted the new girl to go away. Everything had been fine before she'd shown up and ruined it.

"Break it up! Girls, I insist you break it up this instance!" a stern voice said in the background.

It might as well have been a distant squeak, as we were both way too riled up to listen to it. I yanked at her hair, and she pulled back my arm and jabbed me in the face.

"I hate you!" I spat at her.

"I hate you more!" She scratched at my arm.

"Stop this at once!" said another voice, louder this time but still in the background of my rage.

Wrinkled arms fixed around my waist and tried to pull me back. I tried to free myself so that I could pounce on Lisa and continue what I was doing. Miss Braun had her arms around Lisa's waist and was holding her back.

"I hate you!" I screamed at Lisa. "I really hate you!"
I stopped trying to break free. I knew that it was over. I made sure to maintain my venomous look as I looked at the weasel. She continued to try and break free from Miss Braun's grasp.

"I hate you more, you stuck-up snake!" she screamed at me.

"Everyone! Finish your lunch then report to your next class," Miss Braun shouted to the crowd of onlookers.

I watched her drag a still struggling Lisa out of the room. Soon, the rest of the world came back into focus. The shocked looks on the faces of the other girls. Broken plates and trampled trays from when I'd leaped across the table. Spilled liquid and food splattered across the floor. I looked down at myself, and I was covered in bits of food that had stuck to my damp blouse. My hair was encrusted with gross stuff, and I had scratches and bruises scattered across my arms so that I resembled some undecipherable dot-to-dot.

Whoever was holding me, finally twigged onto the fact that I wasn't trying to pull myself free anymore. Besides, Lisa wasn't even in the room. They let go of me, and I turned to see who it was; Miss Crombie's wrinkled old face glared back at me.

"Harper, what is wrong with you?" She tried to brush the food off her arms that had been transferred from me. "This type of behavior is most unladylike and simply not appropriate for a girl of your age!"

I didn't say anything, instead, I looked over at the other girls. Taylor and Amy were looking on open-mouthed, while Sydney had a slight smirk on her face. Before I could stop myself, I found myself smirking too and soon I was struggling to keep in my laughter.

"Come on," Miss Crombie pulled on my arm. "We're going to Miss Braun's office."

I took one look back at the destruction Lisa had caused before I let Miss Crombie lead me out of the cafeteria. I followed her, noticing that everyone we passed was transfixed on me. Yeah, okay, so I didn't look my best, but news spreads fast at this place, so there was no doubt they already knew what had gone down at lunch.

I knew that I was going to be in BIG trouble this time. It wasn't some stupid pillow fight or a few silly initiation tests. I'd not been in a fight before, at least not one like that. I didn't view myself as a particularly violent person, but there was something about the new girl that made me want to scratch and hit her until she disappeared.

Miss Crombie pushed me down into one of the chairs outside of Miss Braun's office and told me to wait there. Here I was again, and I was beginning to feel like I should just move in here. It smelt funny and wasn't very spacious, but it was better than having to share my room with that horrid charity case girl.

I took in my situation and laughed to myself. It was one of those *laugh or you'll cry* situations, and I wasn't one for crying without good reason. Now that my anger and adrenaline had subsided, I ached from the bruises and scratches that the feral girl had caused, especially on the side of my face where she'd slapped me hard. My damp blouse itched at my skin, and the pieces of food I was covered in smelt weird.

Silent, too silent. I didn't like being alone with my thoughts. I preferred to keep myself occupied so that they remained blocked out. My stomach rumbled, and I placed my hands over it, then again, I had only had a couple of mouthfuls of my lunch before that charity case rat had poured water over me. I told myself to relax, and I shouldn't be the one getting into trouble. After all, Lisa was the one who'd started it, not me! Still, I knew that Miss Braun would be furious, and I couldn't exactly faint again to get out of it this time.

Ages passed, I'm not even sure how long. Eventually, the office door opened, and Miss Braun led Lisa out of it. That gutter rat had the cheek to look at me and smirk. I quickly looked away from her and willed myself to remain calm. She wasn't worth it. She was nothing.

"Lisa, go back to your room and clean yourself up and then go to your class," Miss Braun instructed.

"Yes Miss Braun." She nodded.

I sat on my hands so that I resisted the urge to pounce on her. She was such a suck-up! Lisa didn't deserve to be here, she was vile. I hated her! I hated her! I hated her!

"Come in Harper," she demanded in a stern and unfriendly voice.

I followed her into the office and didn't wait to be instructed before I sat down in the chair in front of her desk. She closed the door then let out a long sigh as she sat down in her chair.

"So, here you are in my office once again." She let out a longer sigh. "Go on then, tell me your side of the story."

I paused for a moment and then gave her my sweetest smile. "Lisa hasn't been very nice to me recently. Well, in fact, she's never been very nice. Not even when I came back from the hospital and felt disorientated."

"That reminds me, we never did finish our little chat about the initiation tests you impose on new students." She stared at me. "But we'll come to that later."

Oops! Bringing up my stint in hospital was a mistake! A big one!

"Miss, it was all Lisa," I continued. "All I did was ask her for a glass of water because she was getting one for herself. She poured it all over me, soaking me and making my top totally see-through. She didn't apologize or try to justify her actions. She pushed me to my limit, and I just snapped, anyone would do the same. Lisa publicly drenched and humiliated me."

"Anyone." Miss Braun raised an eyebrow. "I can assure you that I wouldn't have caused such a scene."

"Yes, well you're old," I said without thinking.

"It has nothing to do with age." She glared at me. "It's common decency."

"So, it's okay for Lisa to pour water all over me?"

"No Harper, but she is new here, and instead of making her feel welcome, you have tried to make her endure a silly initiation test and then made uncalled for comments to her."

"So, because she's the new girl she gets a free pass to be as vile as she wants? It seems as though she gets free everything!"

"Enough Harper!" She scowled at me. "Your behavior won't be tolerated in this school."

"But it's all her, not me. Maybe it's because my head is still a little scrambled, but she has been horrible to me since she came to my school," I argued.

"It's not…your school, Harper," she replied sternly. "Did you call her Charity?"

"I just told her that the water is free, she might not have known, after all, she's new here. I was just helping," I pleaded.

Miss Braun shook her head and sighed. "No Harper, you were being nasty. It sounds like you have picked on a number of students at this school. I can't accept this type of behavior anymore."

What did she mean by that? Jeez, all I'd done was defend myself. Lisa should have been the one in trouble, not me. I watched her as she deliberated what to do next. Eventually, she took an address book out of her desk drawer and shuffled through the pages. Seriously, who even had an address book anymore? This woman was from the dark ages. I couldn't help but laugh at this; her eyes instantly fixed on me. I looked down and quickly feigned interest in my nails.
She picked up the phone that was on her desk and dialed a number from her address book. I could hear a ring, ring,

ring.

"Hello Ruth, I'm sorry to bother you, but we've had another problem with Harper," she announced into the phone.

Oh no! She'd called my mother! My mind went into panic mode. This was bad, very bad! My mom was going to be mad, super mad. What if she banned me from coming home for the summer? Or worse, what if she disowned me? "Unfortunately, Harper has been bullying a new girl, and she has been in a fight," Miss Braun said. She was watching me closely as she told my mother. "Do you mind if I put this call onto the speaker so that Harper can participate too?"

Miss Braun turned on the speaker.

"Why are you being so painful, Harper? Who did you bully?" my mom angrily asked.

"I didn't bully anyone. There's this new girl called Lisa who has basically got into here for free because she's a charity case. I tried being nice to her, but she called me stuck-up and a snob. I can't help it if she's jealous of me because I come from a more privileged family than her. I only got into a fight with her because she poured two glasses of water over me and made my top go see-through. They aren't even punishing her mom; they are letting her get away with everything because she's poor."

"A charity case!" my mom shouted. "Miss Braun, do you mean to tell me that you are calling me because a mean little poor girl is harassing my daughter and she had to fight back?"

"Yes but-" Miss Braun started.

"She's just come out of a hospital. I pay for her to be looked after, not to have some poor girl throw water over her. And why exactly is there a charity girl at the school and even worse, in my daughter's bedroom?"

Miss Braun looked flustered. "We have a scheme which allows for one girl a year from an underprivileged background to be admitted here-"

"You allow a charity case into the school for free?" mom asked.

"Harper has also been intimidating new students by making them partake in initiation tests to see if-"

"Exactly what type of establishment are you running? Look, since the beginning of time there have been initiations for all types of things, that is just a little girl prank. I'm super busy, you've got me at a terrible time, I'm about to sign a 20 million dollar real estate deal, and you had better hope it goes through, seeing as I'm paying a lot of money for my daughter to attend your school and your charity girl pays nothing." Mom slammed the phone down.

A look of shock covered Miss Braun's old face. It was safe to say that the conversation hadn't gone as she envisaged it. I didn't even bother to hide my laugh. My mom may have been uncaring and neglectful, but that performance was brilliant.

"Can I go now?" I asked her.

Miss Braun managed to mutter the word, "yes."

I stood up, brushed a piece of dried up food off my blouse and then casually strolled out of the room.

Chapter Eight – Standing My Ground

I returned to my room to find Miss Crombie sitting on my bed. I took a deep breath and shot her a smile. My attention turned to Lisa, who was packing her belongings into her gross old rucksack…result!

I noticed that she'd already washed as she was in a fresh uniform. No amount of clean clothes changed the fact that she was a scruffy mess though.

Both Sydney and Harper were laid out on their beds, Sydney was listening to music and Taylor was reading through her homework.

"Good riddance! You need to know, *Lisa,* that you don't

belong at a school like this. Whether your parents are alive or dead, it doesn't matter, it doesn't change the fact that you don't belong here," I told her with a smirk.

I didn't care that Miss Crombie could hear. My mom's conversation had proved that I was untouchable; there was no way that they wanted to lose my parent's support, let alone their money. I was always going to win out to a girl like Lisa; always!

Miss Crombie quickly got up and stood between us. She must have been worried that Lisa would try to fight me again, after all, that girl was feral.

"I suggest you go and shower, Harper." Miss Crombie glared at me.

"I will, as soon as she's gone." I shot Lisa a dirty look. "She might steal some of my stuff."

Lisa gave me a death stare and finished packing, and then Miss Crombie escorted her out of the room. As she reached the door she turned and looked at me, "I'll get you, Harper. Watch your back! This isn't finished."

I yelled at Miss Crombie, "Did you hear that miss, she threatened me! Throw her back onto the streets immediately!"

Miss Crombie gave me a long, hard stare. "Lisa is staying at this school whether you like it or not. She's being moved to a room with three other *nice* girls. You have a problem, Harper. You are a bully!"

She led Lisa out of the room and had the audacity to slam the door behind her.

"How rude," I yelled, hoping that she could hear me. Taylor looked up from her homework and stared at me. "You certainly are a piece of work, Harper."

Taylor stuck her nose back in her book. I rolled my eyes; her opinion carried no merit. She was a sniveling, pathetic, loser girl.

Sydney didn't say anything. She didn't even look up at me. Embracing the silence, I went and had a shower so I could wash the bits of gross food out of my hair. I rubbed my expensive lotion onto my scratches and bruises, and then changed into a fresh uniform.

I walked back into the room and turned some music on. Taylor didn't look at me, which was great. I didn't want that loser pretending to be my friend if she wanted to side with the charity girl! I wasn't bothered, not one bit. In fact, it was great not hearing her pathetic whining voice. Maybe I should hatch up a plan to get Taylor thrown out of my room too, and then I would have extra space to store my belongings. After all, what was Miss Braun going to do about it, ring my mom? I burst into laughter.

Whether Miss Braun liked it or not, it was me who ruled this school, not her.

Chapter Nine – The Message

So, that was dramatic. As usual, I took a step back and watched from the sidelines. When would Harper learn that diving in head first wasn't always the best option? Although her fight with Lisa had definitely been the best entertainment that I'd seen all year. It was rather funny watching a posh boarding school for young ladies, transform into an animal kingdom. Even funnier was watching Miss Crombie and Miss Braun, two old women, trying to pull Harper and Lisa apart.

What did they expect to happen? They replaced Brianna with a charity case girl who waltzed in here for free. Worse still, they had placed her in a room with Harper. They must have known that Harper wouldn't be accepting of her. Although, in Harper's defense, when she'd found out about Lisa's circumstances, she had been nice to her. That was a big thing for someone like Harper to do, but Lisa hadn't accepted it. Those two girls brought out the worst in each other. If they'd continued to be forced to share a room, then it most likely would have turned into a war zone, with Taylor and me stuck in the middle.

I had to admit that I was relieved to have Lisa out of my bedroom. She brought out Harper's volatile side, and it put me on edge. Drama was great to break the boredom, but only in small doses. Contrary to popular belief I wanted an easy life, with the odd prank thrown in for my own entertainment.

Admittedly, I felt a little sorry for Harper. It was clear that Miss Braun and Miss Crombie had sided with Lisa, but whatever had gone down with Harper's parents meant that she hadn't gotten into trouble. I would have thought that feeling untouchable would have gone to her head, but instead, she seemed downcast. A lot of the other kids chose to be friends with Lisa, and this clearly upset Harper. She wanted to be in charge so badly, but deep down I believed that she wanted to be liked. Kids didn't really like Harper; they were just afraid of her.

Anyway, all this drama had become a little too much for me, so I'd taken to wandering around the school grounds before I settled down for study time. I was walking past the library when the janitor and his cute son Elliot walked around the corner, tools in their hands.

"Oh, hi there Sydney." Mr. Meuler smiled at me. "How's everything going?"

"Good." I smiled back. "Hi Elliot." I looked at him.

"Hi Sydney," he replied.

"It's nice to see you vomit free." I grinned.

The last time I'd seen him had been at the school dance where a drunk Brianna had thrown up all over him.

"Yeah." he blushed.

"That girl got Elliot into trouble. I told them my son doesn't drink, let alone spike a thirteen-year-old girl's drink." Mr. Meuler shook his head.

"Dad." Elliot stared at him.
"Sorry son," he sighed. "It was just very frustrating when I know that you weren't to blame."

"Of course, you weren't, and anyone who says otherwise is a loser," I added. Poor Elliot, as if he would do something like that!

Mr. Meuler chuckled, "Yes, they are."

"Is it true that Brianna left?" Elliot asked.

"Yeah." I gave a solemn nod. "Then we had a charit-, a new girl arrive, and take her bed, but she didn't get on so well with Harper." I grinned.

"That doesn't surprise me." Elliot grinned back, shaking his head.

"Right, work doesn't do itself." Mr. Meuler lifted a hammer. "It was nice seeing you Sydney."

"You too," I replied. I smiled sweetly at Elliot, and he smiled back. He was so cute and the fact that he didn't realize he was cute only made him more adorable.

"Well, I'd better…" He pointed along the corridor to where his dad was already walking off.

I gave an understanding nod and a wave. I watched as Elliot hurried up the corridor and caught up with his dad.

It was then that Taylor and Lisa walked around the corner.

"Who is that?" Lisa looked at the back of Elliot.

"Oh, that's Elliot, he's the janitor's son," I said matter-of-factly.

"He's pretty cute," she said, and my heart sank. Not another one!

Taylor chuckled and then rolled her eyes.

"What! Well, he is…" Lisa gave us a bemused look.

I wasn't worried about Lisa; there's no way Elliot would ever be interested in her. Him liking Brianna was one thing but Lisa…no way! Seeing Elliot was a welcome break from the boredom of this creaky old school.

"Aren't you meant to be studying?" I looked at them.

"Miss Crombie gave me permission to come and get a library book," Lisa commented.

"And she said I could go with her," Taylor added.

"Fair enough." I smiled at them. "I have studying to do, see you later." I waved at them as I walked off.

Harper was going to be so jealous when she found out that I'd seen Elliot. I walked back to my room with a big grin on my face; I couldn't wait to tell her all about it.

"Harper, guess who I saw?" I said as I barged into the room.

Harper was sitting on the side of her bed, sobbing as she looked down at her phone.

"Harper, what's wrong?" I walked over to her and sat down next to her.
"My parents…" she sniffed. "My mom, she just sent me this." She held her phone up to me.

I read the message:
Darling, your father and I are so busy I'm afraid that you won't be able to come back for summer vacation. I know that you'll understand. Lots of love x

"Oh, wow." I sighed. How could they be so heartless?

"Yeah." Harper wiped the tears from her cheeks with the back of her hand. "They really do hate me."

I put my arms around her and pulled her in for a weird sideways hug. Harper's parents were the worst, they were even worse than my parents, and that was saying something.

"It's not so bad, you won't have to go to class, and they put on lots of activities like going to the beach and the theme park." I rubbed her arm. "And you'll get this room to yourself."

"I hate theme parks," she sniffed. "And I hate my parents."

"There will be other girls staying here too." I was desperately trying to think of positive things to say, but it was hard. I would have hated to stay here over the summer vacation.

"Yeah, Lisa, Jesse and that older girl with the weird name." Harper sighed and let out a loud sob. "I'd rather spend the whole summer in here than be stuck with my mortal enemy, Lisa."

I didn't reply. Harper had a point, spending the entire summer with Lisa, didn't sound like an appealing prospect. I chewed on the side of my lip and thought about it…sure, there were people I didn't get along with, I could name a few from my last school. But I didn't think that any of them could be classed as enemies. I'd never jumped across a table to pounce on anyone.

"Everyone else is going to come back with fresh tans and great stories, and I'll be stuck here with her, for the whole summer vacation." Harper's crying increased.

I felt bad for the girl; I really did. My parents were awful, but even they weren't leaving me to rot here over the summer. Instead, we were spending the majority of it in the new holiday home they'd bought back in Venice Beach, which was where I last lived. Apparently, mom was struggling to find a hairdresser as good as the one back there, so that was good enough reason for them to invest in property there. I was rather excited about seeing my old friends Sandy, Rach and Susie. I was even more thrilled at the thought of finally getting out of this place.

I continued to console her as she cried. Her parents totally sucked, far worse than mine ever did.

Harper reread the text message and then threw her phone across her bed.
"I don't want to see them anyway. I hate them!" She burst into tears again and sobbed uncontrollably.

I pulled her into a tight hug and let her cry into my hair. I didn't say anything. Instead, we stayed like that for a long time.

Eventually, she stopped crying, pulled away from me, gave me a faint smile and then grabbed a textbook and started studying.

I walked over to my desk and did the same. It was the final week of school, and we only had a couple more days of exams. I was an A grade student, and I wanted to keep it that way. I knew if I dropped to a B, mom would find that totally unacceptable and I'd be tutored for most of the holidays.

I hated my parents! I really hated them! They'd done some pretty awful things but leaving me in this horrible place with the charity case girl for the entire summer was by far the worst thing they'd ever done. I'd sent dozens of replies begging mom to let me stay at home, that I didn't mind if they were working lots, I just wanted to be there. She thought so little of me that she hadn't even replied. So, I stopped sending any more messages; in fact, I turned my phone off.

I wasn't staying here all summer, no way...even if that meant running away. I'd already hatched a plan in my head. I was going to sneak off when the staff was busy waving off the other girls. I'd catch the bus into town, use my emergency credit card to withdraw as much money as possible, then I was hopping on the next bus to wherever and spending the summer doing my own thing without any adults to answer to. It's not like my parents cared anyway, no one cared about me!

Jeez, history class was boring. Mrs. Alanke no longer showed her inspirational videos at the start of each class, (for amusing prank related reasons) instead she read out an inspirational poem…yawn!

I stared out of the window and thought about my parents spending their evenings dining in expensive restaurants and not giving me a second thought. Before I could stop them, my eyes were tearing up. Oh no, not now, not here! I dabbed the corner of my eyes with my finger and willed the tears back. I didn't want the other girls to see me crying, I didn't want them to think that I was weak.

Sydney stuffed something into my hand. I looked to see what it was; a tissue. I discreetly used it to wipe away the tears and then I gave her a faint smile. I managed to stuff my neglectful parents to the back of my mind and feign interest in Mrs. Alanke's ridiculously dull poem.

"Someone should switch her daily poem for a rap song," Sydney whispered into my ear.

I burst out laughing, which resulted in an instant death stare from Mrs. Alanke. Life sucked, school sucked, everything sucked. But the thought of a sour-faced Mrs. Alanke reading out a rap poem was hilarious.

I was sat opposite Harper at our usual table in the cafeteria, it was pizza and fries which was Harper's favorite, but she'd barely touched it. She hadn't been the same since her mom had told her she wasn't coming home for the summer. I'd tried cheering her up. I'd let her borrow the cute pink top that I'd seen her admiring and I'd made her laugh in history class. It was like she had this cloud of misery surrounding her and regardless of what I said, or did, it wouldn't lift.

Taylor and Lisa walked past with their trays and sat down at the table a couple away from ours. They had changed tables immediately after the fight. Since then, Harper and Taylor only talked when they had to, and Harper and Lisa completely ignored each other.

"Only two more days to go." Amy placed her tray down

next to me. "I can't wait."

Harper sighed and then took a small bite out of the end of her slice of pizza.

"I'm going to Hawaii; we are staying in this luxury villa by the beach. I can't wait to wake up every morning with the sun streaming through the window and step out onto the warm sand. Dad said I can take surf lessons, how much fun will that be! And apparently the boys in Hawaii all look like models!" Amy couldn't stop smiling.

I raised an eyebrow at her, jeez, Amy was totally tactless and unaware. Or was she?

Amy looked at me and cocked her head. Then she looked at Harper. "Oh yeah, you're staying here aren't you Harper? Well, at least you'll have Jesse, Veronique, and Lisa here too."

Harper abruptly stood up and pushed back her chair. "I'm not hungry," she muttered, she left her tray where it was and rushed off across the room.

"It's not like Harper to leave pizza." Amy shrugged before she leaned over and picked up Harper's barely touched slice.

I rolled my eyes. Was Amy really that clueless?

I finished my lunch and feigned interest in Amy's ramblings. At the same time, I was thinking about a mix of final exams, the holidays, and how much it sucked for Harper. I know that we didn't have the best of starts and that she could be super mean at times, but underneath her hard exterior, she was just a scared kid who longed to feel wanted. People who didn't have money longed for it and saw it as the answer to all their problems. My family was wealthy, super-rich in fact, but I looked on at loving families having days out with longing and jealousy. Some things just couldn't be bought.

I looked over at Lisa, and she was laughing at something Taylor had said. She was probably excited about staying here all summer as she probably lived in some shack somewhere. Poor Harper being stuck with her all summer. I was actually afraid that they might kill each other.

"You'll have to come and stay when I'm back from Hawaii; we can have popcorn, watch movies and use the pool. We've just had a new slide fitted," Amy waffled on.

"What did you say?" I stared at her.

"Um, that you can come and stay, I mean, only if you want to. I mean, um, I think it would be fun." Amy gave an awkward smile.

"Yeah, sure." I smiled. "I need to make a phone call," I picked up my gear and hurried across the room.

As stupid as Amy was…she had actually made me think up a brilliant idea. Harper didn't need to be stuck here all summer because she could come and stay with me. Now, all I had to do was convince my parents.

***

I didn't know where Harper had run off to, but it wasn't our room, as I was currently the only one in it. I walked up-and-down the room, my phone in hand.

"You want me to be responsible for someone else's daughter for the entire summer?" Mom moaned into the phone.

"Her dad's a heart surgeon, and her mom's an extremely successful businesswoman." I got straight to the point.

"Oh! Really?" This had perked her interest.

"Yes!"

"Well, um, yes, your friend Henrietta is very welcome here for the summer."

"It's Harper," I corrected her, "And thanks, mom."

"I have a nail appointment to get to. I'll talk to Miss Braun about it later, bye," she hung up on me.

I stared at my phone with a smile on my face. That had been so easy. My mom was such a snob; the prospect of new connections with upper-class people was an offer she couldn't refuse.

One thing was for sure, with Harper in tow this summer was going to be interesting. Now, all I had to do was tell her the good news.

I hated this school almost as much as I hated my parents. I couldn't put off leaving anymore. I was going to go today. I looked around at my secret garden escape, the sky was grey, and it was drizzling, but I didn't care. This was the only place in this old horrible school that I would miss. I leaned back against an oak tree and ran a long strand of grass through my fingers.

I worked through the plan in my head. I would discreetly pack my bag and hide it under my bed, and then I would go to the rest of the day's classes. As soon as the school day finished, I would grab my bag and sneak out before the other teachers left as I knew the main gate would be open then.

My parents couldn't make me stay here. I wasn't going to let them ruin my summer; no chance! I was getting out of here, and I wasn't coming back!

I couldn't find Harper. I looked everywhere, but she had gone incognito. I'd tell her later; she was going to be so excited! Everything was going to be okay. Thank goodness my mom is a total snob!

Right now, I had art class to get too…yawn!

Chapter Ten – Turmoil

I managed to sneak back and pack my bag when my room was empty. It meant that I was ten minutes late for art class, but I invented some excuse about seeing the nurse for a headache. The teacher was far too much of a hippy type to care anyway.

The rest of the day dragged by slowly…really slowly. In the last class of the day, Geography, I played with a globe during the whole lesson. I didn't hear a word the teacher said because I was too busy imagining where in the world I would eventually end up. Australia, Africa, Spain…so many choices. My parents would never find me!

Finally, the lesson finished, and I legged it out of the room so I could go and get my bag. I was getting out of this place, and I was NEVER coming back!

I was going to tell Harper the news after class, but she ran off before I had a chance. Never mind, I'd tell her later.

I needed to take my books back to the library, and then I was going to play tennis with Tiff. I hoped Miss Crombie wasn't on the tennis courts, the sight of her in a short white skirt was enough to give me nightmares.

Luckily, Miss Crombie wasn't on the courts, but someone else was. Yes…Elliot! He was helping his dad to prune a hedge. I couldn't believe my luck!

How should I play this? Should I be super cool and pretend that I don't even see him? Or should I be super friendly?

In the end, friendly won out.

"Hi Elliot, fancy seeing you here," I said, sounding rather

lame.

He looked up and a huge warm smile erupted on his face. "Hey Sydney, fancy seeing you here." He looked embarrassed, he probably thought he sounded just as silly as I did.

"I'm just helping my father to finish this so we can head off on holidays," he said.

"Where is your family going?" I asked. And when he replied, my heart almost stopped.

"Venice Beach, we've got a holiday house near the beach," he said.

I was gobsmacked. I tried to say something, anything…but no words would escape my mouth, so I just nodded.

He then asked me, "Where are you holidaying, Sydney?"

"The same place as you, Elliot," I said in a strangely squeaky voice. "I guess we might see each other there."

"Really! That's awesome!" he replied. He pulled something out of his pocket. It was a pen. "Can I borrow your hand, Syd?"

My heart fluttered, he just called me Syd!

Elliot took my hand and wrote his phone number on my hand. "Make sure you call me, and we can meet up."

"Sure," I replied, trying desperately hard to sound normal. "That's a date. Oh, I didn't mean that type of date. I meant…"

He interrupted and saved me. "Don't worry, Syd, I know what you mean."

His dad called out to him. "Elliot, are you ready to go?"

Elliot smiled and called out that he was coming. "See you soon, Syd." He flashed a huge smile, picked up his tools and ran off.

Oh, how my heart fluttered! I'm sure butterflies were darting around my stomach. He held my hand!! He gave me his phone number!!! Did life get any better than this???

I grabbed my bag from under my bed and took one last glance at my room before I headed for the door. I suppose I'd had some *okay* times here, but the bad times outweighed the good. I wasn't going to miss it here, not one bit!

I'd nearly reached the door when it barged open, and Sydney stepped in. I tried to hide my backpack behind my back and smiled at her.

"I forgot one of the library books I need to take back." Sydney raised an eyebrow. "Why are you hiding your backpack?"

"No reason." I tried to walk past her.

"Harper!" She grabbed my arm. "What's going on?"

"Fine, if you must know, I'm leaving. I'm not staying here for the summer; no chance!"

"You don't have to," Sydney said with a huge smile on her face.

"You can't change my mind, I'm leaving, and I'm never coming back. If you tell anyone, then I'll send you cat mess in the post. My parents don't care about me, so I'm getting out of here and starting a new life where I can make my own rules."

"Where would you go? This is insane!" Sydney asked.

"Wherever, I don't care. Anywhere is better than here."

"What about money?"

"I will withdraw as much as I can, then I don't know, I'll figure something out." I shrugged. "Bye Sydney." I headed towards the door.

"You don't need to leave!" Sydney shouted after me. "You can come to my place for the summer. We will have so much fun together. But you'll have to put up with my anal mother and eat ridiculously healthy food."

I paused and turned to look at her. "You're just saying that because you don't want me to run away."

"No, no I'm not. I was going to tell you earlier, but I didn't get a chance to. I've already asked my mom, and I imagine by now she would have cleared it with your parents and

Miss Braun. You don't have to leave Harper; you can spend the summer with me. My parents have rented a holiday apartment in Venice Beach."

I paused for a moment before I dropped my backpack onto the ground, rushed over to a startled looking Sydney, and hugged her. Tears rolled down my eyes. This was probably the kindest thing anybody had ever done for me.

The door opened so I quickly pulled away from Sydney. We both watched as Taylor walked into the room, tripped over my bag and then shot us a dirty look.

"Who put that there?" she growled.

Sydney and I looked at each other and burst out laughing.

"Whatever," Taylor muttered before she grabbed something from her bed and then left the room.

"We're going to have a great time." Sydney smiled at me. "We can spend all day on the beach and check out some of the designer shops. And you'll get to meet some of my old friends and enemies!"

"I can't wait," I grinned. "Sydney..."

"Yeah?" She asked, smiling.

"Thank you." A single tear ran down my face as I embraced my friend.

Thank you for reading WILD CHILD!!!!
We hope you loved it!
Please leave a review on Amazon.
Katrina and Kaz xx

WILD CHILD
Book 4 - Holidays
Available Now!

Some other books that you may love…

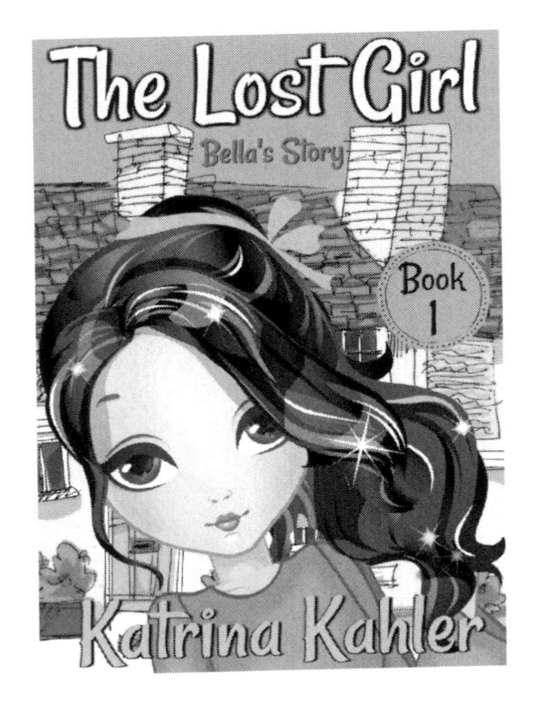

MIND READER
BOOK 1
MY NEW LIFE
KATRINA KAHLER

Twins
1
2
3
Katrina Kahler

Printed in Great Britain
by Amazon